BROKEN ANGEL

Liv B. Newman

Contents

Whenever you need him, he's right here. Protecting and keeping an eye on me. If I don't see him, I still know he's around. I have a strong impression of him. Some people report feeling shivers or catching a glimpse of something out of the corner of their eye, only to investigate and find nothing out of the ordinary. You can put a name to that face, then. In spite of this, it was entirely unplanned that I ended up in his presence. Now that I'm aware of his presence, I've been doing things to anger and frustrate him. I've been calling him out and provoking him, and when he ignores me, I've been putting myself in potentially harmful circumstances in an effort to drive him away. As my personal guardian angel, Gabriel has been assigned to protect me. He protects my physical and mental selves, but he can't keep my heart from him. We are from different worlds, and yet I can't help but fall in love with my broken angel.

Chapter 1

In The Blink Of A Eye

Naturally as human nature goes we take thing's for granted on a daily basis. I'm not just speaking of people, money, jobs, spouse's, I'm talking about the small, unnoticed things. From the sound of a crying baby, the feel of a kittens fur, sand beneath our feet as the ocean breeze cools us, to the pleasant aroma of waking to coffee. Sometimes it takes drastic measures to open one's eye's, to make us see how good we really had it. What I'm trying to say is you don't know what you had until it's gone. So take that as a warning and pay attention. Stop grumbling about what you don't have and appreciate what you do have. Focus more on the smaller things in life, for those are the moment's that will count. Love yourself but not to the point of conceit, but most importantly.... Love life. It can be taken from you in the blink of an eye.

Trust me, I know what I'm talking about. It happened to me. I'm living proof, well not exactly living proof, but I am proof that our lives can be flipped upside down in a nano second. My human name was Evan. Evan Carmichael's. I was the ripe old age of 25, note the sarcasm, when I left this earth. Not of my own doing by the way. Death wasn't how I imagined it would be though. There was no pain,which amazes me considering the way I died. All went black for a few moment's then I was floating, floating away. I saw my lifeless body or my shell that held my soul laying there still as time. At the time I didn't realize I was no more, I assumed it was a bad, but vivid dream, praying I'd wake soon... but I never did. I continued to float away from my body until it wasn't visible, through the ceilings, into the sky up into the star's until I was looking down on Earth. Then I finally woke but not in my bed drowned in my expensive Egyptian cotton sheets. No, I was in a place unrecognizable, a place I had only read about but doubted existed. But enough about that, I wouldn't want to ruin anyone's perception, but I will tell you this... It is wonderfully beautiful.

Now, where I left off... oh right, I had just woken up. I looked like me, sounded like me but I had one very crucial addition. Upon standing I noticed I felt heavier, almost weighted down. Assuming it was due to tight muscles I went to stretch and that's when I completely lost my mind. I heard them before I saw them, a thick fluttering sound followed by a echoing whoosh. Craneing my neck to glance behind me I came face to face with a prominent set of black wings. "What the.." was the first words I uttered which caused chuckles to erupt from around me. Spinning in circles trying to disclose where the laughter came from and fighting to control my balance with my newfound wings was a task. Then several pairs of wings came into view. Some white, some silver, and some black just like mine. Attached to these wings were people just like me, men and women of varying ages. Their smiles beamed down upon me, amusement evident in their eye's. One male with spectacular white wings approached me as I tryed to back away but my wings made me a clumsy idiot. Falling on my rump the winged beings laughed, yet again at my expense. Giving off a sour look at the amusement they found in my confusion one lady crooned. "Oh, don't get upset love. In time you will master your wings just as we did. By the way I'm Belle".

Still dazed and confused I spoke. "I'm Evan".

"No, no, no" Belle shook her head sweetly. "Once here your given a new name love. You leave all remanets of your human life back on earth. You are now Gabriel. Simply Gabriel."

Running a irritated hand through my hair caused my wings to flutter. How the hell do I control these feathers? I thought to myself and giggles erupted again. "It will come in time my dear Gabriel".

Looking at Belle stunned I muttered. "But I didn't say that out loud. How did you...?"

I stopped speaking from just sheer shock. This was unbelievable. Belle gave a gentle smile. "I understand your confused Gabriel, but soon you will understand and it will all come together. Come now, let me introduce you to everyone and proceed with your training."

Within two months I was a wing master. I now controlled them instead of them controlling me. I also learned exactly what I was. I was a angel, but a dark angel, broken, my fate still to be determined. Like I said I was only 25 at the time of my death, I was at the top of my game, loving life, a winner in all things. I was born into a wealthy family and I never knew what a struggle was. I had it all, money, women, cars, clothes. I breezed through school while never cracking a book open. My devastating good looks always won my instructors over and how could they fail such a charmer. Once I graduated at the top of my class no less, I had a job waiting on me at my parents textile company where I was the immediate CEO. My employees were beneath me, being the usual rift raft that slaved away to make my products while not even earning enough to make ends meet. But I had more important things to contend with like was this new chic I was taking out tonight going to let me screw her brains out, or had my high tech surround sound system been delivered yet. There was one way and one way only I dealt with these employees, if they came to me for a raise, ideas, or needing more standard safety equipment I simply let them go. That's right, booted them out on their ass. I had no time to deal with their wants or needs so therefore I saw them as a problem and used the quickest solution to remedy that problem. No matter how much they begged, what tired excuse they used I sent them away straight to the unemployment line. Yes, it sounds bad but I've always looked down my nose on the poor, the uneducated. My attitude was the world owed people like me everything.

I know, I know, your wondering how in the hell did someone like me become an angel, right? Now here's where the All Mighty's sense of humor comes in. Those with Silver wings are retired from the guardian business but oversee us the rest of us. They are our teachers. The white wings are the guardians, and the black wings, which is myself, well we are the test, caught in limbo. My soul wasn't good enough to pass on through, yet wasn't bad enough to be sent downtown. Basically I'm in waiting to receive my mission, a task I must complete to gain my entrance through the pearly gates. However, my task won't be a easy one. I will be made to face my past mistakes and guard a human that I would have once considered a low life alley rat. That's right, see how that works.

Finally after almost two years of hanging out in limbo I received my human to guard and was none to happy. Looking through her file's I seen a headache coming. Alisha Staley was her name. A 23 year old woman child. Opharned as a teen she dropped out of school to roam the streets. Her life now consisted of living in a ruddy apartment in the worse part of San Francisco, working as a tattoo artist in some grimy palor. Her free time was spent sleeping her life away and if she wasn't sleeping she was partying it up, drinking, drugs, and sleeping around. Clearly a version of my human self but only poor. She wasn't hard on the eye's either even though her hair color seemed to change a lot and her make-up was a bit dramatic. Clearly she is what you call one of those grunge girls, gothic I believe. Judging from her choice of clothing you couldn't determine if she was going to war or apart of a medevil play. But that's the least of my worries, Alisha seems to live a dangerous life with all the drinking and dabbling in drugs. She lacks self care and will be the first to throw a punch. Now it's my duty to save her soul, cater to her wellbeing, and lead her in the right direction, without showing my presence. Yes, seems unbeatable but Alisha will learn no matter what. She won't be the reason I'm stuck in limbo forever, she's my one and only ticket to uptown and I won't allow her to blow it. Reciting the three rules that we mustn't ever break,

1. Never expose yourself

2. Never cause harm to our human

3. Do what's necessary to protect them

Now I must prepare for my earthly descent and wrestle Alisha's demons.

Chapter 2

Story Of My Life

"Freaking fantastic, just what in the hell have I stepped in" I grumbled aloud as I lifted my left foot up to inspect the sole of my shoe in the middle of the sidewalk. I didn't care who had to maneuver around me or that I was holding people up. "Ugh... just gross". I hissed as I encountered a stringy, sticky piece of gum glued to the bottom of my shoe. Finally I stepped aside and scrubbed my shoe on the side of a building to work the gum off. It was around ten at night and I had just left my job back at Inktastic tattoo shop where I was a artist. Thankfully it was a Monday night and things were slow. Not too many drunks out wanting to get inked up during the week like on weekends. We stay slammed during the weekends due to vacation goers wanting to add ink to their adventures.

Anyways the night wasn't over for me. I was on my way to my favorite place, The Dragon's Lair. A cool, dark club where people like me fit in. After a few rounds of Yagermister, a fat blunt, maybe pop me a little X, and find a willing partner to give me a quick fuck. Thankfully I have tomorrow off and can sleep my hangover away before I go out and do a repeat.

Let me clear a few things up first. I wasn't always like this. My mom died when I was twelve from a brain annerism which left me and my dad alone. My dad was a good man. He worked his fingers to the bone in some mill making car parts. The pay wasn't the best but we had food on the table and a roof over our head. I was a straight A student going into my senior year and a month away from turning eighteen. My heads were always in the books planning my future out. Unlike my parent's I had high hopes and dreams and my dad gave his all in supporting them. My intentions was to attend UCLA on a scholarship I was sure to be awarded. I'd never had a boyfriend, not because I was dog ugly, plenty of people often commented on my beauty. I just focused on my schooling more than anything and didn't won't the headache a boyfriend was sure to bring. The few friends I had were just like me, nose stuck in the books. We wasn't like most teen girls out here flirting the guy's up, going insane over the newest fashions or gushing over a pop music heart throb. No, our girls night consisted of discussing the inner workings of an atom, debating the latest political scandal, or cramming for a exam. Excitement was a nonexistent word in my vocabulary but that's how I liked it. I was a straight laced never bending arrow with my eye on the target... get educated, land a good job and move my dad as well as myself from the slums. But the hand of fate stepped in and my world came crumbling down around my feet.

No matter how long it's been, I'll remember that day for the rest of my life. It's my first thought upon waking and the last thought before succumbing to a alcohol slumber. Like I mentioned earlier my dad was a factory worker that established car parts. He'd been employed there since I was a toddler and was proud of his work. It was a rainy, cold, fall evening when he walked in and collapsed into a kitchen chair burying his head into his hands. Concerned I asked what was the matter. In a strained voice he replied "I lost my job today".

Shocked, I sat beside him and muttered "I don't understand. How?"

Giving a deep sigh he said in a tired voice. "Seems the bosses son that took over the other year thought my suggestion of supplying us with rubber gloves to keep the wires from stabbing our fingers was a waste of his time, so he canned me".

"But dad, he can't do that". I shrieked in anger.

Surprisingly my dad raised his voice at me and banged his fist along the table. "Well he can, and he did".

Sensing that my dad was in no mood to discuss the loss I gently patted his shoulder and tried my best to soothe him. "Don't sweat it dad, something will come about. I can even get a part time job to help out".

Rising from the table he looked at me with sorrow in his eye's. "Thanks hun. I think I'm going to call it a night. I love you more than you know".

Bending down he placed a kiss atop my head and gave me a squeeze. The defeat and sadness was evident in his eye's. "Love you too dad".

As he made his way out of the kitchen he turned to me and said. "Promise me you'll get out of here and make something of yourself".

Nodding my promise he gave me a weak smile and disappeared to his room. That was the last conversation I had with my dad. The following morning I woke and started my usual morning routine to prepare for school. Noticing my dad wasn't up yet I went to check on him. When I opened his bedroom door a scream shattered the morning bliss as I sank to my knees. There my dad was, swaying slightly from his closet with a belt looped around his neck. My dad, the only person I had, the only person who loved me had hung himself leaving me alone in this bitter world.

This is what changed me as well as my outlook on life. I was sad, scared, but most of all angry. How could he leave me all alone. Didn't he love me enough to stay? If he wasn't strong enough to stay and face his demons, I would break ever promise ever made to him and that's what I did. Since I was basically a few weeks shy of eighteen there wasn't much the state could do about me choosing to stay at home on my own. I never returned to school, instead I got a job as a truckstop waitress. Even with my earnings it wasn't enough to continue living in my home, and honestly I hated it there. It was nothing but a vessel of bad memories and broken dreams. Instead I found a low rent one room apartment deeper in the slums. Soon my life dramatically changed more so. I met people of the wrong caliber, that led to partying, drinking and drugs with a lot of sex. I can't even recall the night I lost my virginity or to whom. Turns out I had a artistic eye and that's how I landed my current job, even though I probably want hang around long. Yep, I have a track record for abandoning jobs.

College was long gone right with my dreams of a education. I was content and happy with my life as it was. My friends were my vice along with Jim Beam or whatever liqueur I could afford. Sometimes though memories of how my life once was would worm their way into my thoughts and I would take long walks through the woods to soothe my soul. It was in those woods I could be my true, old self, out of the scrunity of other's eye's.

That's where I remember the girl I locked away deep inside, recall my dad's laughter, our small but cozy home and for a second I wished for it all back, but the rebellious me would resurface and squash those thoughts.

Kinda like having an angel on one shoulder and the devil on the other. Both whispering what I should and shouldn't do. Not to surprisingly, the devil always won sending the angel fluttering away. No one can save me…. I'm too far gone.

Chapter 3

Wicked Imagination

Anyways I entered my loyal hangout and headed to my usual spot at the Dragon's Lair. I don't know why I always chose to sit on this lonely, secluded bar stool at the corner of the bar but I did. Something about it was comforting. All the usual patrons knew this was my spot as well and left it empty in my wait. Hopping atop the stool I grabbed a handful of peanuts that graced the bar in small dishes as a complimentary. Jason, the bar keep grinned when he noticed me and called out. "It'll be the usual for ya?"

"Not tonight Jay, I had a amazing day at work. Go ahead and top me off a bit of yager". I laughed.

It wasn't long before my friends had joined me and we kept the drinks coming inbetween tearing up the dance floor. By one I was three sheets to the wind and was realing digging some guy, I think he called himself Chad, but I didn't care at this point.

Coming on strong I was throwing myself hard at him and allowing his hands to roam my body, basically I was encouraging him to do so. Slinging back another shot I smiled up at him through my lashes trying to be as seductive as possible but I was never graced with the talent of being sultry. I was somewhat a natural clutz, my hair was long and right now colored a silverish blonde. To be honest I dyed my hair as often as I changed my underwear. Blonde today, purple tomorrow maybe. Anyways it didn't take to long for me to convince this Chad character or whatever his name may be to accompany me to the bathroom. Once there we passed around a dooby then I let him screw me against the bathroom stall. Neither of us didn't give a hoot who waltzed in, we just continued our business while giving them a show. Once finished we went our separate ways, which was how I wanted it. I never stuck with the same guy for fear of attachment. All that love and relationship garbage isn't for me. I've never been in love nor had a orgasm. That's right, I'm probably the only 23 year old that's never had their world rocked. But it doesn't matter to me, sex, drugs, drinking, it was vices to me, made my pain numb.

Grabbing another shot of yager I saw my friends from across the room and gave a farewell wave. Stepping out into the crisp air I knew I was in no condition to walk home but hailing a taxi seemed to be to much of a struggle. Once they took in my stumbling drunk form they sped on by. Nobody wanted to contend with a drunk. Making my way down the sidewalk I hummed to myself as my body zig zagged to it's on beat. I was two blocks from home when suddenly I was jerked into a dark alleyway. Too drunk to understand what was happening I laughed up at the two burly men welding knives in my direction. "Give us your money" the smallest of them growled at me.

Busting out laughing I said between hiccups. "I can't. I drank it all up".

Reaching out he grabbed my hair and curled his filthy fist into it. Placing the knife at my throat he nodded to his partner. "You see him girl?"

My only reply was a grunt. "That's my buddy and your going to do whatever he likes and then when he's done your gonna give me whatever I want and if you don't they'll have to search in a different location to find your head. Got it?"

Honestly I was to drunk and high to realize the danger I was in. I knew something wasn't right yet at the same time I didn't care, I laughed. I recall feeling my shirt ripped open and hands groping at my body but what happened next had to be a figment of my drunk imagination. The men had already shoved me down onto the garbage strewn ground and the one that had threatened me was between my legs raising my skirt up. Then just like a gust of strong wind had whipped through the man positioned between my thighs was lifted and thrown back several feet into the air. He landed with a thud against the dumpsters. His partner assumed I was the cause of this but no, no human had that type of strength. His partner went to pummel me with his fist but his blow stopped midair, as if he had frozen stiff. A look of confused terror filtered over his features as I watched through my drunken hazed eye's as his hand seemed to bend at the wrist at a very unusual angle. It seemed like he was doing it himself as he yelled out in pain as his wrist snapped. Screaming out he looked down at me in awe and stuttered. "Your the devil, spawn of satan, you witch, evil woman".

Running over to his partner he helped him up as they both hauled ass away from me and out of that alleyway. Snickering to myself I tried to stand up and that's when I saw it. A tall muscular man dressed in black jeans and a hoodie. There was something about him, it was like just by looking at him my body was filled with a calming peace, I felt suddenly sober. Strangely I didn't feel threatened by this odd man, instead I felt warm despite the cold breeze, I felt clean despite all the drugs and alcohol in my system. My vision was no longer fuzzy or that of a intoxicated person. For the first time in a long time I could see clearly, think clearly. Then I have no clue as to why but a image of my dad surfaced and he was crying. I knew this image was only in my mind but why was I picturing my dad crying? I gazed back up at this stranger prepared to speak but as I did all the air was sucked from my lungs at the image I saw. Attached to this stranger's back was a large set of black wing's, magnificently beautiful. Due to my cleared mind I felt a surge of fear and let out a ear splitting scream, but before it could leave my throat his hand clamped over my mouth and the sweet scent of pine needles and ocean breeze enveloped me. I was going under, suddenly sleepy. I battled my fluttering eyelids to stay awake but then he soothed me. Tracing his finger along my cheek he cooed "shhhh".

Smiling lazily up at him, I cupped his chin and mumbled "you are so beautiful" as my eye's lost the battle and sleep overtook me.

Chapter 4

Accidents Happen

The passage back to earth was almost liked being sucked through a whirlwind cyclone. This spinning tunnel of grey tossed me about like a popping corn kernel then landed me with enough force in some alley in San Francisco, my hometown as well as Alisha's. If I was still human the impact would have definitely crushed my bones. Standing up my feathers were ruffled, and I do mean literally. Giving my wings a good flap to correct them I brushed the crumbled concrete from my clothes. That's right, I landed so hard and considering my strength I cracked the pavement. Taking my first step on earth sense my untimely death I felt forlorn, saddened, depressed even thinking of all I lost. I would have been 28 now but sense angels don't age I'll forever be stuck at 25. As I approached the sidewalks I was a little in awe at how people scurried right pass me not knowing I was there.

Then something even stranger occurred to me, the smell of earth. It wasn't the usual smell of pollution that smogged the skies, or the earthy scent from the ground, tree's, and flowers. I couldn't even smell the delicious aromas that wafted from restaurants. No, what I smelled was odd, unexplainable, a stench so thick it was overwhelming. So many scents mixed into one, sour, sweet, flowery, burnt rubber, onions, honey, just so many. Unfurling my wings I flew high in the sky, above the buildings, into the clouds. Only there could I breathe in fresh, clean air. Pure air, and that's when it hit me, I wasn't smelling garbage, loud perfumes, or smog, I was smelling people's sins. If it was a pleasant smell the person was rather decent, if their smell omitted a foul oder their soul was dark, doomed. Floating back down to earth I focused on getting my senses under control. Closing my eye's I concentrated on one person at a time and within a hour of walking about I had it down.

Me, always having been michevious and up to no good decided it would be fun to exercise my powers. Not just to annoy people but to experiment with my power. Leaning against a building I waited for my first suspect to stroll by. A middle aged lady happened by and I tap her on the shoulder. She turned in my direction then I tapped her on the other shoulder. She looked so befuddled I snickered to myself and moved along. Next I saw a business man walking briskly along in his expensive tailored suit and stuck my foot out tripping him up. Of course I caught him before he pummeled to the sidewalk and he stood there for a moment trying to figure out what just happened. My best was yet to come, catching sight of a hot chic, one that I would've hit on had I been human, got the shock of her life. As she passed me I smacked her on the ass. Turning abruptly she saw no one. As she resumed walking I smacked her rump again which sent her into a fearful Sprint. Laughing I decided it was time to stop playing and get on task.

Walking along I finally seeked out this tattoo parlor where Alisha worked. Looking through the grimy windows I didn't see anyone but a lady behind a counter sporting a fire engine red mohawk and multiple body piercings. Disappearing through the glass I passed her and noticed she was looking over a biker magazine. Just for sport and because I could, I flipped the magazine shut and grinned at her bewildered expression. Moving on along I crept down a smoky, dimly lit hall that had tiny rooms on each side. Glancing in the first room I saw a man having his nipple pierced, the next was a girl having ink work done and so on. Finally I found what I was looking for at the last door on the left. There she was, Alisha. Bent over the back of some leather wearing older man with a long beard that would make ZZ Top proud, she was working her needle magic.

As I inched closer I saw that ironically she was working on a image of hell across his back. Then that's when it hit me, a scent so powerful yet soothing. Breathing in deeper I could determine it was lavender with a hint of vanilla coming off her. My mind immediately remembered my mission, I was here to save her soul before it was too late while earning my way in. Focusing back at the task at hand I stood behind her bent over her shoulder watching her work. Suddenly she stopped and gave a small chuckle as she rubbed her neck. "Sorry Chuck, I had a crawling sensation on my neck". She said to her client.

Resuming my post behind her I had to know if she had felt me. Ever so softly I let a slow puff of air float out from between my lips and attack her neck. Chuckling again, she stopped her work to grab her neck. "Hold on a second Chuck. I need to pull my hair back. Seems it keeps tickling my neck".

I had my answer, she could feel me. Satisfied, I backed off and let her work. Even though she was a bit odd there was a certain beauty about her, almost a beckoning of some sort which I found strange. Never in my human life would I have took notice to someone like her. As I was off in la la land Alisha pulled away from the man to retrieve more ink. As she turned she hesitated right in front of me and tilted her head up and stared directly into my eye's, or where my eye's would have been if she could see me. It seemed like she could see me or maybe sense me, I don't know. Alisha remained there for a moment staring at me before shrugging her shoulders and continuing her work. After that I just relaxed against the wall until she was finished.

Trailing in behind her I followed Alisha to a suspicious looking bar and that's where I saw the real Alisha, the careless girl I was suppose to save. Irresponsible, I don't give a fuck attitude sat on her shoulders like a trophy she was proud of. It was clearly obvious all this was a act, trying to chase her demons away through self abuse. As she led a stranger into the restroom I waited in the hall not wanting to invade on this private moment, or what should have been a private moment. Obviously Alisha didn't care who waltzed into the bathroom to witness her sexual escapade. This girl is living a dangerous life and if it takes all I have I will set her on the right path. Alisha will not be the reason I'm denied entrance.

Afterwards I assumed she was headed home so naturally I'm by her side because I am her guardian angel After all. Of all the billions of humans luck would have it that I got stuck with a delinquent. As I floated along beside her I sensed trouble ahead. Trying to sway her into changing her route was freverless. Up ahead two dead beat, good for nothing men stepped into our pathway. The stench that rolled from their oily bodies was foul. Rotting food mixed with the worse case of morning breath ever assaulted my nostrils. Pushing the smell aside I focused on my main priority... Alisha.

It was clear what their intentions was and Alisha was so drunk and strung out she didn't have the mental capability to fight back. Within a flash I lifted the man that had crawled atop her off. His weight was that of a feather compared to my supernatural strength. Slinging him up in the air I effortlessly tossed him into the dumpster rendering him unconscious. The other guy tried to run fearlessly but was no match for my speed. I was on him before he could get two steps in. During this chaos I hadn't realized that I'd became visible until the guy uttered up at me in complete shock. "I I, I. Your not real, y-your not real".

Letting my black wing's spread I released a low growl and the man ran off. I decided he wasn't worth the chase and turned my attention back to Alisha. She was setting up with a goofy smile on her face, I'm assuming trying to make sense of what she was seeing through her drunken haze. Walking toward her slowly I bent down to her level. Alisha's smile widened and she cupped my jaw with her tiny hand. "Your so beautiful" she muttered before passing out. Wrapping my arms around her I slowly lifted her up above the buildings and flew us to her apartment. Tucking her into bed I kept watch over her.

My mind was worried what tomorrows outcome would be. Would she remember me or think I was a drunken vision? If she did recall what she saw how was I to handle it? The most important thing was to learn to control my emotions and senses better to avoid such mishaps. During my rage I lost control and therefore my identity was revealed.

Chapter 5

Only In My Dreams

"Gurrrrr" I groaned as I started to wake and streached like a large, lazy cat. Grabbing my alarm clock off my nightstand I pulled it closer to bring the bright red numbers into focus. I don't even know why I have the thing in the first place, it's not like I've ever set the alarm to get up. Seeing that it was 12:43pm, I shoved the clock back and flopped like a fish over to my stomach trying to force myself back into sleep, but strangely I felt rather chipper. Laying there staring into my purple pillow-case I was amazed I wasn't suffering from a hangover after last night. Usually after a night of spirits I suffered the next day, but there was no headache, no sour tummy, no sensitivity to light. I felt good, body, mood, and all. I can't recall the last time I felt this good. If I didn't know better I would say I was happy.

Finally crawling out of bed I trudged to the fridge and grabbed the carton of milk taking a big gulp. Replacing the milk I took another good stretch and stripped from yesterday's clothes and tossed them in the corner along with the huge heap of other dirty clothes, which reminded me I needed to do some laundry. Prancing around naked I turned my bluetooth speaker on to full blast blasting my current favorite punk band. Then I turned the shower on full blast and as I was waiting on the water to warm up I heard a loud knocking on my floor along with some incoherent words being yelled. Naturally I knew it was Mr. Harris, the old man who lived under me. Frustrated because he didn't share my appreciation for music, I stomped back on my floor and yelled. "Turn your hearing aids down you old coot", then I lowered the volume. Finally I jumped into the shower without testing the water and hissed as I pulled my body back. "Son. Of. A. Bitch. I think I just boiled my skin off". I squealed.

Once I had the temperature pleasant I began to scrub my body until I hit a sore spot on my back. "Owww" I howled out twisting my body into a deformed pretzel trying to investigate what was up with my back. "The fuck is that shit?" I questioned myself as I saw a angry scratch and bruise. Then it all came tumbling down on me like a ton of bricks. "No fucking way" I gasped.

Getting off work, getting hammered, screwing what's his name, walking home, two men attacking me, a beautiful angel with dark wings coming to my rescue, I replayed through my muddled memories. It's not possible. I must have really been sloshed and smoked some good shit. It was a dream that's all. Even though I can't recall how I got home or where the scratch came from I knew beyond a doubt it was only a wild dream.

Finishing my bath, I toweled off and sprawled across my unkempt bed naked lost in my thoughts, trying to piece together last night's event's. Eventually my stomach knocked on my ribs reminding me I needed substance. Hopping up I opened my fridge only to see the milk, last week's leftover sub that was sure to be spoiled, and one egg. Tossing the sub into the trash I glanced around my apartment and noticed it needed a cleaning. The dishes were piling, trash reaching it's limit, and I probably had one clean outfit left to my name. Sliding into a long, cotton, flowing black dress, paired with my clompy black combat boots I headed out the door. My first stop was a ruddy diner that served the best burgers this side of town. After gobbling my meal down I strolled along the sidewalk to my favorite goth boutique and splurged on a new belt. I was on my way to the market when I passed the alley I visioned in my dream. Stopping I looked down the trashy pathway and curiosity got the best of me. Deciding to snoop on in I looked around for any signs that my dream was actually a reality. Feeling silly after seeing nothing I turned to go and that's when it caught my eye. Just the tip stuck out from under a old newspaper but it was clear what it was. Taking the toe of my boot I nudged the paper away to reveal a rather large black feather. Squatting down I picked it up to further inspect it. A trickle of anxiety eased up my spine but I shoved it off. Standing up I whispered to myself. "It's just a coincidence".

For some reason I couldn't force myself to toss it back down so I stuffed it safely into my bag. Looking around once more I backed out of the alley and continued to the market, pushing my thoughts aside. After purchasing a few items to ensure I wouldn't starve, I opened the door to leave and it slung closed very quickly and was about to smash my fingers when suddenly it stopped, just like that. Not all the way opened yet not closed. Tilting my head at this strange occurrence I moved my hand and watched the door close ever so gently. Staring at the door I decided to test it again. Swinging the door open I placed my fingers back in the danger zone and sure enough it stopped before crushing my hand. Once again I pushed the door open but this time I didn't place my hand in harm's way and the door shut completely. I stared awkwardly at the door until I noticed some snotty woman watching me as if I was a freak show. Sending her a sweet angelic smile I slowly raised my hand and unfurled my middle finger. "Didn't anyone ever teach you it was rude to stare?" I chirped.

Looking appalled she hastily sauntered off with her nose up-turned. Giggling to myself I continued on my way. Once at home I stashed all the strange happenings away and attacked my apartment with a mop and broom. After running my dirty laundry downstairs to use the community washers I began cooking my dinner. After eating I remembered the feather and retrieved it from my bag. Inspecting it closely I brought it to my face and ran it down my jawline to my neck where I busted into a fit of giggles from the ticklish trail it made. Running it across my hand it felt as if it was made of silk, definitely not a normal bird feather. Placing it atop my dresser I dug my phone out of my bag to do some research. I estimated the feather to be about two feet long. Okay Seri, work your magic I thought as I asked. "Birds that have two foot long black feathers"

Seri brought up a few pictures of birds and none were native to San Francisco, much less America. I combusted into laughter once again as I pictured a ostrich running loose in the city. No, no, I really need to find out what I took last night because I sure am wigged out today. Giving up my search I turned my attention to other matters... watching the latest episode of "Lucifer".

Streaching out on my bed I got comfy and within moment's I was snoozing.

Chapter 6

Flash

My day zoomed by and before I knew it, it was time for me to report for work. I hadn't given anymore thought to the recent occurrences, it just seemed better to not think about it. I have never been one to really believe in ghosts or other supernatural mumbo jumbo and besides who would want to haunt me. I mean my life is so dull a spirit would even feel sorry for me. Everything that has happened recently is just a coincidence and workings of my overactive imagination. It was time to get a grip and put all that hogwash behind me, and I had done just that until I got to work.

Soon as I got there a customer was waiting on me so I tossed my coat and bag aside and scrubbed my hands. Snapping on a pair of latex gloves I entered my booth. Inwardly, I rolled my eye's as I saw a repeat customer who seemed to never learn. Sasha was a victim of her own ignorance but I just kept my trap shut and gave her what she wanted, After all she was paying my bills. At least every three months she skipped in here with her bubbly self and dingy personality. Don't get me wrong, she was a sweetpea and a delight to work with, she was just to gullible when it came to men. She would gush over her newest boyfriend and share stories of how in love they was and they had goals. Demand that I permanently stamp his name on some part of her body while covering up the last boyfriends name. So far I had done this four times in the course of two years. So, here's a tip people... Don't get your lover's name tattooed on you unless you've hit a major milestone, like maybe three to five years. No, I'm lieing, I've actually covered up love tattoos on people that was married for years. Do what you want by all means.

Anyways I plastered a fake and very rare sunny smile on my face. "What can I do for you today Sasha?"

"OMG!! Alisha I have finally met the one. He's going to marry me and we are going to live Rome, well after he leaves his wife and all that is".

Squinting at her stupidity I questioned. "His wife?"

"Yes, I know it sounds horrible but she's really a witch to him and treats him like garbage. Technically their already separated and he sleeps on the couch. He's just waiting for the right time to tell his kids".

"Ohhh". Was all I could say as I turned away to hide my "you dumb bitch" expression. "So Sasha, what can I do?"

Giving me a cute smile she purred. "I want his name on my left tit".

"No problem. What's the name doll?"

"Eugene. Oh and can you cover up Tanks name with a unicorn?"

Tank was her latest mistake. Some muscle bound douche that was so full of himself. "I sure can".

As I got started on the newest name I asked mostly to be friendly and make conversation. "So what happened with Tank?"

"Humpf.. I caught that bastard with his personal trainer, who by the way is a man".

Stifling my laughter from her outrageous life I sadly shook my head and muttered. "Life can really screw us sometimes".

At the mention of screw Sasha went into a full blown, detail oriented conversation about the hot sex she shared with her newest flavor. Tuning the majority of her chatter out I only nodded and replied when necessary. I mean I really didn't need to know about his obsession with stuffing her vagina with various fruits and vegetables. That was just an over share.

Thankfully it didn't take long before I completed her work and as always I took a picture with her in support of my art. I did this with every customer and put them on the outside bulletin board to draw more clients in. Once she was gone I embraced the silence of the room as I playfully banged my head on the wall. It had been a busy night and was after midnight when I was ready to go. Gabrielering my belongings I entered the lobby where Silvia, the desk attendant was engrossed in some game show. "See ya tommorw Silv". I called as i gripped the door handle. "Oh wait". Silvia screeched in her very nasal voice.

"Yes" I said turning around.

"I have the pictures of you and your clients today. Do you want to display them before you go?"

"Nah, I'll do it tomorrow". I said turning to go once once more.

"But wait Alisha, there's something you need to see".

Knowing I wouldn't get out of here until I gave into her pestering, I sulked over to her desk relunticaly. Silvia scattered the photos out amongst her desk. Glancing at them in a rush to leave I didn't see anything that stuck out from the normal. "I don't see anything unusual".

"Look closer Alisha".

Biting the inside of my cheek in irritation I gave a closer look and that's when I noticed a soft yellowish glow hovering beside me in all the pictures. Shrugging it off I spoke. "Probably just a reflection or something like that".

Silvia shook her head causing her tight red curls to bounce. "No girl, this isn't a simple reflection showing up in all these photos. It's a orb".

"A what?" I asked sarcastically

"A orb, a spirit of some sort. Could be a ghost, angel, or demon".

She let the word demon roll off her tounge slowly and threatening. Busting out in laughter at her seriousness I said between guffaws. "That's just absurd. I don't believe in any of that mess".

Yes, I was lieing, mostly because of the recent happenings and admitting to it would make it real. Silvia gave me a stern look over her spectacles. "I'm serious Alisha. Things like this do exist. You need to do your research".

Nodding my head in hopes she'd shutup I agreed. Swiping the photos up I stashed them into my bag. "I'll bring these back tomorrow okay?"

Finally I was out of there and my heartbeat was erratic. Canceling my plans to stop by the Dragon's Lair I rushed home. I knew exactly what I was going to do. Once inside my apartment, I bolted my door shut and tossed my bag onto my bed. Getting on my knees I looked under my bed and pulled several storage boxes out. These boxes contained some of my dad's belongings as well as my childhood memorabilia. Flipping the lid off the first box I rummaged through it but didn't find what I was looking for. It took me until the third box to end my hunt. Pulling my dad's old Polaroid camera from the box I felt like a magician. Pushing things aside I found some film and loaded the camera. This camera would give me a different perspective than a phone camera. Holding it out in front of me I took a few selfies and let the pictures fall to the floor. Next I took various shots around the room. Finally satisfied, I Gabrielered the pictures from the floor and shook a few that hadn't developed yet. Feeling as if I were going crazy I settled down at my small breakfast nook to examine the shots. Sure enough there was the same exact glow in every portrait. Standing up I could feel the hairs on my neck prickle as I glanced around my room. "Where are you?" I muttered.

Nothing.

"I know your here. Show yourself you bastard"

Nothing.

Getting angry I stomped my foot. "I'm not afraid of you and I'm telling you now to leave me the hell alone whatever you are. I saw you once, you and your black wing's. Show. Yourself. Now."

Still nothing.

"Why are you here? What do you want with me?"

That's right, nothing.

Getting overly worked up I was about to start tearing my pad apart to find some answers when I felt a calming warmth come over me and a soft tickle on my neck. Standing still I whispered. "Is that you?"

Chapter 7

This Little Light Of Mine

Yes, you can tell I'm rather new in the Angel business considering I keep messing things up, or may be Alisha is just too observant and not the dead head I thought. This chic misses nothing, better than the damn FBI. At the store the other day her fingers were in jeopardy of being crushed so I intervened, so she decides to play a little game of open-shut with me. I had no choice, I couldn't let the door crush her hand... or could I?

That's not the worse part though, the worse part is how she prances around her home always in the buff. At first I turned away and try not to cop a look but that's hard when the majority of the time she's nude and just maybe there's a bit of human male still buried in my angel soul. Alisha has a amazing body and it's a shame she hides it beneath those black, bulky clothes she chooses and allows men to use it. But enough about all that, I have a major issue occurring at this very moment. I've screwed up too many times and Alisha knows something isn't right plus she's a smart cookie. The way she whipped that old camera out and shot over a dozen photo's you would have thought she was in a showdown in the wild west. There was no way I could zap myself out of every portrait, she was just too fast. Now she stands in the middle of this crappy apartment demanding I reveal myself.

I'm going to give her what she wants. Yea, so what I'm breaking the Angel rules, won't be the first time. Plus I have a feeling that, that will be the only way to get through to her. Alisha is a very strong willed woman and it's going to take more that just flying around her head to set her on the straight and narrow. It's time to scare her straight. Stepping closely in behind her I released a tuff of air against her delicate neck. I saw her posture stiffen and a inch of uncertainty cross her features before she whispered "Is that you?"

Grinning at the ways I could really mess with her head, I opted against it. After all this isn't some little game nor a time to be a joker. Placing my lips right next to her ear I whispered like the wind. "Yes".

Laughter erupted from deep within my chest as she jumped like a frantic cat and skidded to the opposite side of the room.

Glancing in my direction she stuttered out. "W-what do you want? W-what are you?"

Gaining control over my amusement I spoke in a soft yet deep tone. "I'm here to save our souls".

Her eye's flipped from side to side urgently trying to locate my whereabouts. "O-our souls". Alisha repeated more or less to herself.

"Yes. Seems you are on the wrong path in life. I'm here to correct it and in return gain my passage. I mean no harm".

I sensed a change in her demeanor, almost as if she were suddenly angry. "I don't need any help. My life is perfectly fine, the way I like it, so you can just go back to wherever it is you came from".

"Tsk, tsk, tsk. It's not that simple Alisha. I'll be by your side until you recognize your wrong doings. Only then will I go".

"Why can't I see you? Show yourself, don't be a coward".

"I'm far from a coward little girl". I said beside her ear once more and watched her scurry to the door. I beat her to it and held it shut. "Let me out. You can't keep me here".

"That's where your wrong Alisha. I can do whatever I wish. Now calm down and let's have a reasonable conversation".

"No" she spat. "Not until you show yourself. If you want my cooperation let me see you".

Letting a breath of frustration out, I knew I had to do this to gain any ground with the irritating woman. Concentrating all my engery into my core I made myself visible. Raising my head to meet her astonished face she froze. Her jaw hung open like a loose shutter and she slowly brought her hand up to cover the gaping hole her mouth displayed. "You asked, I gave it to you".

After a hard moment Alisha slowly made her way toward me. Tilting her head at ackward angles to absorb every inch of me she finally came to a stop mere inches from me. With a shaky, slow movement she brought her hand to rest on my chest. With a gasp she quickly retrieved her hand as if I had shocked her. "What was that"? She inquired bewildered.

"What was what?"

"When I touched you I felt a buzz, almost like a electrical current running through you filled with warmth".

"It won't hurt you, it's just the feel of my blood coursing through my body, my feelings, my inner workings".

Before I could continue she placed her hand back on my chest but this time left it there. As if that wasn't enough she placed her free hand on my upper arm. A dizzying smile cracked her lips open as her eye's closed and her head tilted back. "It feels so good, like a humming running through me. I feel so happy, so safe, soooo good."

Taking notice of her increasing breaths, and redened cheeks only one thought occurred to me. Could she be on the verge of a orgasm just from touching me? Her thighs clamped together tightly and her tounge licked at her moist lips. "It's, it's getting stronger. Oh it's so nice".

Her grip tightened on me and I knew I had to put a stop to this. Roughly I removed her hands and a sad whimper escaped from between her puffy lips as I took several steps back. "Do not touch me again without my permission".

Alisha's lusty smile evaporated like steam as she glared daggers at me. "What did you do to me?"

"You did it to yourself Alisha. As I said, never touch me".

Stepping closer to me again she asked. "What are you?"

Rolling my eye's at her dumbness I simply snorted. "What do you think I am?"

Taking a moment to reply she spoke. "You look like a dark angel, fallen, broken".

"Correct".

"So your evil".

Laughing at her stereotyping of me, I shook my head no. "That's what television has made humans think but it couldn't be farther from the truth. To answer your question, no I'm not evil. Quite the opposite to be exact."

Alisha reached toward my wing so I quickly darted out of reach. "Don't touch me".

"B-but your feathers are like no others. There almost like silk, so soft".

"You must listen to me Alisha. I'm here to help you, not seduce you."

Giving up on trying to touch me for the moment she asked. "Do you have a name".

"Gabriel".

"Gabriel". She whispered so sweetly.

"Yes, Gabriel. You know it rhymes with math, bath, and so on".

Shooting a hard look my way she snarled. "Yes, I know. I'm not stupid".

"Good, I'm glad you cleared that up. However judging by your behaviour I'd have to beg the differ".

Rage filled her eye's and her body took on a defensive stance. "You know nothing about me".

"Wrong again sweetheart. I know your a tattoo artist, both your parents are gone, you like to party too much and screw strangers in bar bathrooms while other's watch. I also know you like to walk around here in your birthday suit".

Sucking in a deep breath she hissed. "You've watched me naked? You pervert".

"Call it what you want Alisha. Now that you know maybe you will keep your clothes on and your legs crossed. I will be by your side at every turn you take. You can't escape me, not until you wake up and cherish your life".

With that said I vanished before her eye's.

"Gabriel, are you still here?"

"Always."

Chapter 8

Silent Stalker

Just what in the hell am I to do? I mean this is some out of world shit I'm dealing with. I'm still not totally convinced this is really happening, I'm just twisted up in some odd nightmare. You couldn't even call this stalking, no this was more like a kidnapping. I'm being held hostage by some paranormal oddity. I can't even see him which only worsens my delima. It's not like I can report this to the authorities. They would surely give me a one way ticket to the crazy house and throw away the key. I'd be the next wacko plastered on the Enquire but instead of the headline reading I was abducted by an alien, it say kidnapped by a dark angel. If I truly didn't believe I was losing my mind I'd laugh at all this rubbish. Right now, the point is that I need to figure out how to make this angel disappear for good and fast.

Not going to lie though, he was a looker. It's scary that a angel makes me want to commit sins, but he is just scrumptious. Dark, thick hair, nicely built, the most piercing blue eye's paired with his olive toned skin. Just plain yummy. Not to mention that strange sensation that overtook my body as I touched him. It was like his hands was on every part of my body at the same time, no spot left unattended. I could feel a humming thrill vibrate down to my bones. My mood and emotions instantly changed, going from scared and worried to peaceful and wanting. Fuck I'm not even a happy, smiley person, so I guess just his mere presence brought out the best in me, made me happy, and giggly. That explains my chipper mood over the past few day's. His golden glow is rubbing off on me and I don't like it. I can't continue to rebel if I'm all happy and shit. Yes, Gabriel must go.

Now he's just reveled he knows my entire life history as if it's a best selling novel, but he's full of shit. He can't know my deep, darkest secrets, the reason I'm like I am. More power to him if he think he can change me. I'm bound and determine to prove him wrong, as a matter of fact I know just the person I can talk to. Silvia. She knows all about this sort of craziness. That's right dear Gabriel, in a few days I'm going to send you back to cloud nine. Be prepare because I'm going to serve you up on a silver platter and devour you.

First thing first though, how to speak to Silvia if Gabriel is constantly latched to my side. Then it hit me. Ahhhh.... the ole mighty higher power of a text message. First thing in the morning I'm hitting her up. As for now I've got to figure out where he's at in my apartment. Pushing my thoughts aside I cleared my throat and called out. "Hey feather man, would you kindly disclose your whereabouts and stop playing all this Houdini crap?"

Several seconds passed in silence then suddenly I hear a loud "Boo" echoed in my ear. Jumping like the devil himself had appeared, I balled my fist up and yelled. "Stop doing that shit, will ya? You can't just go around sneaking up on people".

Hearing him chuckle only infuriated me more but I pushed my anger aside. "Seriously, where are you?"

"Sitting right beside you".

Looking in the direction of his voice I mumbled. "Wow, you really don't believe in personal space do you?"

"Until your fixed, your space is my space".

"Why don't you expose yourself so I can at least see where you are?"

"No can do. It's against the rules. I only did it earlier so maybe the seriousness of your situation would sink in."

"Okay, so what if I was in danger, would you expose yourself?"

"Depends on the situation".

Nodding my head I made mental notes to use against him later. Then another thought occurred to me. "I have some ground rules as well".

Hearing the sigh he released I had no doubt that he just rolled his eye's. "Please Alisha, let me hear your rules"He said with sarcasm.

Ignoring his smartness I made my demands. "When I shower, dress, etc. You are to leave me alone in privacy. You must become visible so I'm assured your not perving on me"

"Whatever Alisha. By the way you should stop wearing all those baggy clothes. You have a tight little figure that should be showed off".

Gasping at his rather unangelic remark I retorted. "And tell me exactly how you can save me if your making comments like that?"

"Oh I can. Just watch and learn. Watch and learn kid".

Tired of his arrogance I stood up. "Goodnight" I grinded out and fell into my bed.

The next morning as I ate breakfast I sent a text to Silvia.

"How do you get rid of a unwanted spirit, demon, and the sort?"

I wasn't about to let her know why I was asking because the last thing I needed was everyone knowing about my craziness and Silvia was sure to blab.

"What are you doing?"

Jumping and tipping my coffee I squealed. "Didn't I tell you not to do that shit. Now look at the mess you've made. I thought you was asleep, or even better....gone".

"Sorry sweetness, I don't need sleep. I'm always up. By the way do you know you make this adorably irritating chewing motion in your sleep?"

Tossing my spoon in the direction of his voice I hissed. "Are you even watching me while I sleep, that's just tenth degree creepy".

"Hey, like I said I don't sleep. I needed entertainment".

"Then watch t.v., read a book, fly off a cliff for all I care".

"Wow, anger issues much?"

"No. Your just cramping my style and I don't like it".

"Newsflash Alisha, your style went out a decade ago. All the 90's grunge bands called and want their wardrobe back".

"Oh, ha, ha, ha. That was a good one you over grown bird. Now kindly shut up and let me be".

"Right after you tell me who you was texting".

"Silvia about some work issues".

He seemed satisfied with that answer and I continued my breakfast. Finally Sivial text back with what I needed to know. Salt I had, sage was another thing though. Slipping my shoes on I headed for the door and I could feel Gabriel's presence around me. I went to the closest market and got my sage along with a few other items as not to look suspicious. Once at home I grabbed the salt from my cabinet and went to the center of the floor where I spread it out in a circle around me. Then I lit the sage with a lighter and swished the smoke about. Supposedly the salt circle would keep him from me and the smoldering sage would expel anything harmful from my home. After a few minutes I heard Gabriel making a gruntal sound. "No,oh no, I'm melting, I'm melting. Help me".

Everything went silent and I was shocked that this seemed to work. Just as I was getting ready to rejoice I saw the salt circle being scattered wildly and the smoldering sage being put out. Laughing he spoke. "You silly little thing you. That mess doesn't work Ghostbuster. Like I said your stuck with me. Suck it up buttercup".

Yes, i truly felt stupid and couldn't even argue back over my idiotic tactics to rid me of this annoying ass. "I'm taking a shower. Expose yourself like we discussed."

A second later his beautiful black wing's came into sight along with the rest of him. Rushing over I yanked one of his feathers out just to get a bit of revenge. Walking toward the bathroom I heard that bratty chuckle of his.

Chapter 9

Enough Is Enough

For the remainder of the day Alisha chose to ignore, especially after her little salt and sage incident. Which was by all means fine with me, less stress and chatter. Naturally I trailed her to work later that day and no matter where I was in the room it seemed her eye's always found me. After work she made her way to the Dragon's Lair. Before she opened the door I whispered in her ear in a warning tone. "You shouldn't go here. This place isn't good for you".

Giving the door a jerk she hissed. "You may be stuck to me like a leech but I will continue to live my life as I please".

Storming into the bar like a lunatic on a mission, Alisha sat down heavily on her usual stool tucked into the corner of the bar. Sticking her hand out to grab some peanuts, I quickly swiped the bowl off the bar sending the peanuts crashing to the floor. Setting a fixed glare in my assumed location she whispered hissed. "Real classy asshole. Leave me be and let me enjoy my-self".

Fine. If that's what she wants I'll give it to her...this one time. After tonight the ballgame changes. Alisha will see just how much I can control her. I had hoped I wouldn't need to use forceful tactics but she asked for it. For now I'll let her live it up but come tomorrow she's going to see exactly why I am a dark angel. Yes, sweet little Alisha is in for a shock. Leaning down I nearly pressed my lips to her ear and gritted out in a lethal voice. "Have fun tonight, for it will be the last time".

I was already across the room before she could reply. Setting back in a sour mood I watched as she drank and slipped off to the bathroom once again with a total stranger.

Alisha made it home around three in the morning a intoxicated mess and passed out on her bathroom floor. Soon as the clock hands touched 8am I became visible and set out to do my work. Flipping the shower knob, I blasted the cold water on. Lifting Alisha up, I none to gently deposited her into the tub. Several high pitched screams echoed throughout the bathroom as she ripped the shower curtain down in her struggle to get out. Finally free she stood there in her drenched clothes and teeth chattering. "Why did you do that, you pompous asshole?"

Laughing despite myself I answered. "You needed freshening up".

Alisha switched the hot water on and with a growl shoved me from the room then slammed the door in my face. I'm sure she heard my deep laughter which only fueled her anger more. After a bit she came out with a oversized fleece robe and her hair wrapped up into a towel. Soon as she saw me a sour expression marred her face and she stomped to the coffee pot. Regardless if she hated me or not I was here to do my job, so might as well get my speech out of the way. "Alisha, all your wild nights, meaningless sex, drugs and drinking ends now. If I can't get you to see that your carelessness choices has your soul in danger and encourage you to make changes I will forever be stuck in this limbo. We can do this the hard way, or you can just give living clean a try. The choice is yours, but let me warn you... I can make your life a living hell".

Downing her coffee in one gulp she got busy making another cup as she mumbled sarcastically. "What do you know about being human"

That did it, I was sent over the edge. I let my anger erupt and acted before I could control it. Focusing my energy on her ceramic mug, I watched as it basically exploded in her hands. Shards of glass scattered everywhere along with the coffee. Alisha let out a shriek but before she could react further I gripped her arms and due to my anger the current that emitted from me wasn't pleasent. It wasn't the warm, fuzzy feel of ecstasy, no this was rather like shock waves. I could see the uncomfortablity surge into her blue eye's that was now harbouring unshed tears. Still I didn't release my grip. Instead I yelled much like a roar. "I know alot you lost little girl. I was human up until three years ago when some animal decided to end my life. I had it all, loved life, and because of one stupid decision on my part, I lost my life. Do you know how that feels? Of course not, but your heading down the same road like a freight train that has jumped the track's, and trust me, the place your going isn't pleasant. I've seen it".

Seeing the tears spill over onto her pale cheeks and trying to worm her way out of my grasp, I finally released her. Alisha ran her hands up and down her arms massaging the pain away. Feeling a tinge of remorse, I offered a gruff apology. Then what happened next came as a surprise. Alisha whispered a calm "sorry". In that tiny second I saw the girl she once was. There was true innocence and sorrow in her eye's, but just like a flash it was gone and this fake Alisha was back. Storming to her bed she plopped down and buried herself under the covers and spat. "At least if I'm sleeping I'm not out there screwing up".

She had a point there, but still I felt like shit for losing my temper. After cleaning up the broken mug and coffee I took a seat on the broken down couch and stared into the outdated box television set that still had bunny ears attached. Assuming the wicked witch had fallen to sleep it startled me when I heard her voice. "So you use to be human?"

Hoping my little tantrum may have been groundbreaking I sopke. "Yes".

"Will you tell me about it?"

Honestly I didn't want to relive it by dragging it up, but if it helped my cause then so be it. "I was 25. I had it all. Money, awesome job, woman. The finest of the finest things. My life revolved around money and material possessions. The more I had, the more powerful I felt. Different, higher class woman all the time. Love was for the weak, or so I thought until I met Cassidy. Falling fast and hard made my common sense fly out the door. Cassidy was only interested in my money was engaged to some rough neck want to be tough guy, Brantly. I tried everything to convince Cassidy to leave him, be mine only but she refused. Cassidy claimed she loved me but couldn't leave him. I had to have her though at any cost so I kept up sneaking around with her. I had taken her to a nice dinner and we caught a show. Afterwards we headed back to my place and I was pouring us some wine when my door burst open. In came Brantley swinging a gun. Cassidy immediately went to his side as he sneered at me. He asked Cassidy if he should kill me." I paused because this is the part of the story that was the hardest to tell. Taking a ragged breath I continued.

"I'll never forget the coldness in her eye's when she said go ahead, I don't care what you do. Brantley took aim and everything was in slow motion. I watched as the bullet swirled at me and imbedded into my head. Oddly there was no pain, no noise. I was calm and peaceful and that was it".

When I heard no response from Alisha I looked over and saw her now sitting in the middle of her bed, tears running down her face at my tale. In a hushed voice she spoke softly. "I'm so sorry Gabriel".

"You have nothing to be sorry for".

A few moment's in silence passed before Alisha spoke again. "Was he caught?"

Slowly I shook my head no. "My parent's put everything they had in hiring the best of best investigators and worked closely with law enforcement. In the end they skipped town and left no evidence behind. Also my parents never knew about Cassidy, no one did. Basically I left them no leads".

"Do you know where they are now?"

"I use to keep up with them but stopped. It only made me suffer more. Last time I checked they was in New Mexico working on a ranch."

"That's so sad Gabriel. Can't you use your powers to avenge your death or point the athuorties in the right direction?"

"Yes, I could but I'm not allowed to intervene. Fate has to handle them. My parent's never let my apartment go. It's like some type of shrine to them. If I had my life to live over how I'd do things differently."

Looking over at Alisha with her sad look I spoke. "Let me help you Alisha. Don't be the next me".

Snuggling back under her blankets she gave a small smile and said "I'll think about it".

Nodding, I wasn't going to argue further at the moment. I felt like it took a lot for her just to agree to think about and after me telling my story I felt like I had chipped away at her wall a bit. No need to press my luck though.

Chapter 10

Take Me To Church

So yea, hearing Gabriel's story did melt some of the ice away from my frozen heart. I really did feel for him. No one should go that way and at such a young age. After hearing his tale apart of me wanted to tell him about my dad and why I'm like I am, but talking about it makes it all too real. Plus I know Gabriel knows most everything about me, but he doesn't know why I do what I do, that I wasn't always this out of control, careless girl. I had dreams and goals once upon a time. It's just being hard and nasty prevents me from feeling and if I can't feel I can't be hurt.

After work that night I headed straight home instead of dashing to the bar. If Gabriel was surprised he didn't say anything. As a matter of fact we haven't spoken since our outburst this morning. In fact, I'm not even sure if he's still here. Maybe I finally ran him off with my wicked ways and sharp tounge. Relaxing in a hit bath for a bit, I got out and slid my jammies on, popped some popcorn and grabbed a soda. Plopping on the couch I tuned into a rerun sitcom show. The gnawing at not knowing if he was still here was unnerving though. I had to know.

"Gabriel" I whispered.

After a moment's silence I heard his gruff yet sensual voice. "Yes".

"I was just wondering if you was still here? You've been so quiet".

"Yea, well I figured you could use a little space".

Nodding my head, I patted the couch. "Come join me, watch a little tube and warp our minds".

He didn't answer but I knew he did because I could feel his weight bare down on the couch. "Could you make yourself visible please? It's strange sitting here feeling something beside you yet not seeing it".

Within a few seconds his black wing's sprawled out behind him and he resituaited himself on the couch. I found a good action movie on the t.v. because I wasn't about to make him set through a chic flick. The silence was killing me and this wasn't like him. "Are you okay?"

"Just watching the movie". Was his only reply.

"Okay fine, I give. If I agree to give this living right thing a try, will you stop acting like a moping fuddy duddy?"

Gabriel grinned. "That would be wonderful Alisha, however this is one of my favorite movies and I'd enjoy more if you didn't feel the need to talk".

"Ooo-kayyy". I said amused. He snickered and turned his attention back to the movie. Action flicks wasn't really my thing but I managed to sit still. Midway through I started getting chilly and gave a litter shutter. Gabriel glanced at me and I felt his wing ever so gently slide in behind me. Immediately warmth enveloped me and I felt at ease, peaceful, content. I could feel the currents he emitted buzzing, but this time there was pain, nor did it feel sexual like the first time I touched him. It just felt good, cozy, safe. Not being able to control myself, I curled up further into his wing and relished in the silky softness, better than any fur or fleece blanket. Without warning, I fell into a blissful slumber.

I was awoken by Gabriel strumming my hair with his fingers and whispering in my ear. "Let's get you to bed. Movies over."

Blinking my eye's open, I noticed my head now rested on his lap and my arms encircled his waist. His wing still covered me. "Sorry". I mumbled as I slowly released him and sat up, sliding away from his warm glow. I was instantly chilled again and all my problems came rushing back. Bidding him goodnight I went to bed.

When I woke the next morning I felt awesome. No hungover headache, no fuzzy memories. My head felt clearer than it had in a long time. I almost felt like the girl I use to be. Looking around I didn't see Gabriel so I decided to let him be for now, especially after embarrassing myself from having had fallen asleep on him last night. Hopping from the shower I decided to slip into a pair of jeans I haven't worn in years and a normal t-shirt. Skipping my makeup I opted to go natural today. Going to the kitchen I grabbed a yogurt and granola bar for breakfast and called Gabriel out.

"We are going on a walk this morning".

A few seconds passed and Gabriel appeared. He still seemed a tad odd to me and I couldn't understand why. Shrugging it off I went to the door as he vanished again but I could feel his warmth beside me. I went to a local park that was in a country setting. Walking toward the treeline, I spotted the overgrown path and stepped in. After several feet in the tree's blanketed us from view. You was in a entire different world out here away from all the hustle and bustle of the city. Hidden from life, if just for a bit. "I think your safe to show yourself out here". I told Gabriel, and there he was suddenly looking glorious in this woodsy setting.

I admit I was gawking. It was like this dark angel belonged out here amongst the darkness of the tree's. So beautiful to look at, like a painting or scene from a movie. Gabriel spoke breaking my trance. "So where are we going?"

"A special place." Is all the information I gave him. Soon we broke into a meadow filled with white and yellow wild flowers. In the center there it stood still proud, boasting sanctuary. A old, rickety, wooden church. The boards gray from age and the paint long gone. Holes evident in the roof and the bell tower slowly crumbling, but to me it was magnificent. As we entered the time weathered church the wooden floors creaked. Gabriel asked. "Is this place safe?"

Smiling I had to. "Safer than the Dragons Lair".

He gave me a smirk as I led us to the sturdiest looking pew. Taking a seat the dust rose up around us getting a sneeze from me. I broke the silence by saying. "There's something I have in common with this beaten down church".

"What's that?"

"It was left abandoned too just like me, forgotten".

That really got Gabriel's attention and he looked at me as I continued." I've known about this place since I was a teen, long before I lost my dad. I use to come here often when it felt like the world was against me. I came almost everyday the first month I lost my dad and strange as it may sound I felt at ease, at peace and safe. Also close to him. Even with it in ruins like this it's the most beautiful thing I've ever seen. It's a shame it's in this shape".

Pausing to look around at the millions of cobwebs that decorated every corner I had to know. "Have you seen my dad, you know up there?"

Gabriel sadly shook his head. "It doesn't exactly work like that Alisha".

"Is it as beautiful as some say?"

"Even more so".

Suddenly I giggled. "I was saying how me coming here and my reasons why was strange, but what could be stranger than sitting here chatting with an angel".

Laughing together I kept talking. "So how long will you stay?"

"Until I'm convinced that you've changed".

"And I'll never see you again?"

"No, but I'll still look in on you from time to time even though you'll never see me again. I'm here on a mission only. You had a guardian angel before me and you'll be appointed another one after I go".

Eventually we headed back to my apartment and later that evening Gabriel told me it was his turn to show me something. Taking his hand in mine he disappeared and led me through the busy streets. Finally he led me through the gates of a cemetery. I didn't question him, I just let his hand tug me around. He came to a stop under a lone willow tree that had one nice headstone resting there. I read the name and date but waited for him to speak. By now the sun had vanished and the sky was dark. Gabriel appeared and looked down at the stone. "This is where I lay".

"Your name is Evan?" I whispered.

"No longer. Evan lies here and Gabriel is the new me".

As he stared down at the cold stone his jaws tightened and I could tell this was very painful for him. Taking his hand I gave it a squeeze. "I'm so sorry this happened to you, but thanks for bringing me here and sharing this with me".

Gabriel only nodded so I stepped away to give him some privacy. Looking at this beautiful dark angel I knew right then I would bring his killer to justice no matter what I had to do. They would no longer walk around free after what they did.

About an hour or so later Gabriel said let's go. Nodding my head I took off walking but he pulled me back into him. To say I was surprised was a understatement. My chest was crushed against his and his arms held me tightly. Before I knew it I was being lifted off the ground at a rapid pace. Screaming I looked down and saw everything getting smaller and smaller. Burying my face into his chest I gasped. "Gabriel what are you doing?"

"Taking you sight seeing from a different perspective. Open your eye's and look".

Shaking my head no I gripped him tighter. "Relax Alisha. I want let anything happen to you".

Giving in I peeked out and gasped. We were in the clouds. "Holy shit". I blurted out and heard Gabriel chuckle. Getting brave I raised my head further up and was stunned at the beauty around me. Once I was comfortable enough Gabriel turned me around so my back was against his chest so I could take in everything. His wings made this tantalizing deep swoosh sound that was re-laxing. Seeing him in flight was just as beautiful as the sights. He started to fly lower and came to rest on a tall steel pillar of sorts. Releasing me I rejoiced at having my feet back on solid ground until I realized I was standing at the very top of the Golden Gate Bridge. Feeling swimmy headed I reached for Gabriel and he was by my side instantly. "Have a seat until you adjust".

He helped me take a seat then sat behind me wrapping me in his wings. I leaned back against his chest and let his buzz warm me while looking out. I could see the night lights of the city for miles and it was breathtaking. Twisting my neck to look at him I was prepared to speak when the very soul of my world was rocked. As I parted my lips to talk Gabriel snatched me closer to him and pressed his lips to mine. I've never felt anything so delicious, so satisfying in my life. This was no ordinary kiss, this was heavenly. His current seemed to vibrate into my bones, covering every inch of me and suddenly I wanted more, so much more.

In that moment I had never been kissed, until I was kissed by my dark angel.

Chapter 11

Murderer

What the hell am I doing, what am I thinking? I just kissed Alisha. I'm not supposed to do that, this isn't suppose to happen. I'm not even human but yet I still get yearnings that of a male human. This is impossible. I'm here strictly on business so to say, not to seduce the poor girl. I very well may have just blown this entire mission, but as I pulled my lips from hers and gazed into her sapphire eye's filled with lust, I knew it was worth it and I'd do it again. I want to do it again. Right now I want to smother her with my mouth and do so much more to her. Alisha deserves to know what real love feels like and I can show her.

Thunder sounded in the far off distance and angry clouds seemed to be moving in rather fast. Yep, that's my sign, their way of telling me I have made a royal mistake. There's no going back now, no rewind button on this mess, but I'll take whatever they throw at me. I wouldn't take it back if I could. It's funny how life works, I thought I was in love once with Cassidy but all that was just a sham. This, this right here with Alisha was real and I couldn't lose her ever. I have fallen hard for this twisted, tough cookie, but I know the inevitable will come, the day she's strong and I am called home. As for now I will pretend Alisha is mine If only for a little while.

Noticing that Alisha's lust filled eye's had dimmed and uncertainty was crossing her features I ran my hands slowly up and down her arms to calm her. "You kissed me?" She said slowly.

It wasn't exactly a question but more of a statement. "Yes I did".

"But we shouldn't, I can't, your an angel, we can't do this". I smiled at how flustered and confused she was as her thoughts ran rampant through her mind then she spoke again. "Or can we?"

It was if she was thinking out loud and her thoughts was at war with right and wrong. Laughing at my bundle of cuteness I gave her no more time to mull it over. Lifting her up to my lips I picked up where I left off. This time something snapped in Alisha and she met my firey passion with a smoldering passion of her own. She cradled my head in her hands and if was if she was trying to get as deep as she could in my mouth. I was aware my current was at a high and I knew she could feel how badly I wanted her but when she moaned out I knew I needed to back off before my current overtook her to much and sent her sailing into a unforgettable climax.

Once I pulled away I noticed during our steamy session that I had started floating with her in my arms. We were no longer standing atop the bridge. Tucking a strand of hair behind her ear I said in a deep voice. "Let's get you home angel".

Arching a amusing brow at my new nickname for her she agreed. Once home it didn't take long before she was snoozing doing her adorable little chewing motion. She probably fell asleep quickly because my current had drained a lot of her energy. I was heading to the couch when a strange sensation overcame me. If was if I was going numb and feeling weak. Then right before my eye's my body started breaking up into tiny particles, almost like a scene from a scifi movie. Soon I was totally evaporated. I couldn't see myself but I could feel myself in a jelly type state. It wasn't long before all these particles came together again and I was complete, whole, but I was no longer in Alisha's apartment. With one glance I knew where I was at and Belle came into view with a look of dread. In a blink she was in my face and hissing. "What are you doing Gabriel? You know the rules. You know any emotional connection is prohibited".

I just stood there and watched her normally brownish gold eye's turn to yellow flames as she continued. "You very well may have cost that poor child her soul and blew your second chance as well".

"But I love her" I said meekly and that was the only defense I had. For a split second I thought I saw remorse flicker in Belles raging eye's. Calming herself she spoke curtly. "I must speak to the higher up about this. I shall return".

Like a gust of wind Belle vanished and I waited which was torture of it's own. Not knowing what was going to happen or what to expect next. After what felt like eons Belle ghosted back in. Giving me a fixed stare she spoke with command. "You are to return and lead Alisha to righteousness. However I must tell you some truths. Do you remember her father?"

"No, should I?"

Placing her hands on my temple she projected a memory into my mind. Horror struck me and if I was human I'd would have lost the contents of my stomach. This simply couldn't be. The man I fired over safety equipment was Alisha's father. I'm responsible for his death as well as Alisha's ruined life. I'm just as guilty as the man who took my life. Even though my hand didn't kill him my actions did. I was a murderer.

"I'm ashamed" I whispered.

"The fates for you have now changed my dear Gabriel". Belle spoke.

"You will continue to save Alisha's soul but you must tell her the truth. You must tell her how you played a role in her father's untimely death. If she chooses to forgive you and continues to love you, you will be granted admittance to the other side. If she chooses the ladder, you are doomed".

Breathing in deep I accepted my new fate. I knew this truth would crush my Alisha and I hated to be the one to hurt her. I wasn't even sure if she loved me and if she did was her love strong enough to forgive me. Even if she couldn't forgive me and I was doomed I would without a doubt make sure her soul was saved, even if it cost me mine.

Chapter 12

Winging It

That bridge moment though. True, I've never been one to idolize romantic gestures... that is until I flew in the clouds and shared a kiss with an angel atop the Golden Gate bridge no less, with city lights as far as the eye could see. That moment right there gave me a entire new perspective on the whole boyfriend love mushiness. Gabriel just set the bar for any men in my future, really who can top that.

When I thought about my future that's when my love bubble popped. Gabriel would be returning, leaving me behind. I can't fall for an angel for so many different reasons. After he's gone then what, where does that leave me. I tell you where it will leave me...heartbroken and feeling abandoned yet again. Life is so unfair, in my case anyways. Never once have I had feelings for a guy and the first time I do it's for someone unattainable. Yes, I can have him for now, but not always.

Pushing those depressing thoughts aside, I focused on my newest mission, finding Gabriel's killer. This was going to be hard to pull off considering he's always around, but where there's a will there's a way.

Looking at my clock I decided to pull my lazy carcass from the warmth of my bed and get this day started. Once showered I skipped out of the bathroom to find Gabriel visible on the couch. I stopped in my tracks when I saw the sullen look on his face. Offering a bright smile I spoke. "You okay?"

Lifting his eye's to mine he returned the smile and shook his head. Spreading his wings out he motioned me over. Scooting next to him I curled up in his wings and arms. Softly I stroked his silky feathers as I asked if he was okay again. A simple nod was the only answer I was given. Worry overcame me as I assumed he was regretting last night. Pulling from him I stood up and said. "It's fine, I understand. Your upset about kissing me last night and wondering how to get yourself out of this predicament without hurting my feelings. I'll make this easy for you, I'm okay, no feelings hurt here. All is well".

With that I rushed to my coffee pot but before I could make it I was swooped off the floor. Gabriel had me in his arms and floating in the air. "Alisha you are so far from the truth. I regret nothing about last night". And as if to prove it he captured my mouth in a feverish kiss. Before I knew it I was laying on my bed with Gabriel atop me. The sight of him on top of me with his wing's above was very erotic. A thing that fantancies are made of. His smooth muscles rippled with every move he made and that delicious current he emitted was divine. Even though I was laying down I felt as if I was floating, so content. I'm usually a dominant lover but with him I just wanted to relent, let him be in charge. Giving in I raised my arms above my head in surrender, giving him full permission to do with me as he pleased. Gabriel noticed my submission and I felt the curve of his lips as he smiled into our kiss. My shirt was being raised up and as his hand neared my breast I felt the hum of his current which made my nipples swell to tightness. This was unbelievable, he could just hover his hand above my body and the currents would send gratifying tremors through my body. He hadn't even touched me yet and I was mewing like a kitten as tiny sweat beads budded on my upper lip and between my breast. Giving a knowing chuckle, Gabriel tugged my pants down and the vibrations was just too intense. Crying out, I bucked my hips up to him. As he trailed his hand away my thoughts wandered, if the hover of his hand caused this, what would it be like when he entered me. My thoughts was scattered as he did just that. Biting down on my bottom lip I tried to extinguish my scream of pleasure. Peeking up at his glorious face, he brought his wings down to cradle me and the current only amplified. His hips were rotating in a tortuous rythem causing a intense grind against my sensitive button while sliding in and out of me at a dangerous pace. Finally my climax rained down and continued to rain down. Never had a orgasm lasted this long. I was feeling it from my head to my toes. Arching my back I clutched his shoulders and gave in to my screams. In this moment I only knew one word in the English language and that word was Gabriel.

Afterwards I fell into a peaceful sleep, my energy depleted. When I woke Gabriel was still by my side. Yawning, I stood up on wobbly legs and prepared for work. The evening whizzed by and I was suddenly aware of exactly how to get the info I needed on Gabriel's killer... Silvia. She was a expert on things like this. Honestly she should be a detective or work for the FBI. Later that night I pretended to be surfing the net as I shot a e-mail to Silvia. I explained that I was interested in Evan's cold case and gave her all I knew on the subject. I also told her to only contact me through emails and never discuss it at work or by phone. I wanted to see this through before Gabriel had to leave me.

That night I slept like a baby in the arms of a angel.

Chapter 13

Time For Change

Have you ever done something so wrong but it felt so right? How can something that feels so right be so wrong? These are the questions I wrestle with on the daily since our relationship took a serious sharp turn. Several weeks have passed since the night Gabriel and I first made love. Since then we can't keep our hands off each other. We've turned into that icky couple I use to cringe at, you know the one's who are all "I love you, no I love you more" using cutsey pet names, and all touchy feely. Yep that's us. Naturally we can't go out on dates in public so Gabriel goes above and beyond to make it up. Some nights we just lounge on the couch watching movies and others he flies me about the night skies, or to the tallest landscapes. Whatever we do it's always perfect.

Also I've done a lot of changing as well. I actually laugh and catch myself smiling these day's. I'm more friendlier toward other's and I haven't used alcohol or drugs in awhile, nor visited the Dragon's Liar. I dyed my hair back to it's original color and added more color to my wardrobe. Not because Gabriel asked me to, no he actually liked my Goth self. I did this for me. I'm trying to get back to the girl I use to be, the one before tragedy struck. Not just my looks, but I also enrolled myself into college. Of course I still work as a tattoo artist because I have bills to pay and I gotta eat. All I can say is that I'm utterly and truly happy with my life at the moment. I'm Happier than I've been in a long time.

There's one thing I do know for sure is that I am totally in love with Gabriel. I never dreamed that love could be so intense, leave me so full and sedated at the same time. My biggest fear is how I'll go on after he leaves and I know it's coming and there's nothing either of us can do to stop it. I'm trying to think positive about it like it's better to have known a love like this to not have known it at all.

In the meantime Silvia came through on her search for Gabriel's killer. I have there whereabouts and amazingly it isn't far at all. Seems they assumed everyone had forgotten about Evan's murder and returned. Even stranger is the fact that they live less than a block away. On a important note though, how was I to tell Gabriel I found them and how he would react to this news but I could withhold it from him any longer. We had just sat down to a movie and Gabriel pulled me up against his side by using his wing. I decided to bite the bullet and get it over with and done. Sitting up straighter I took his hands and looked at him. "I've got something to tell you"

Turning the t.v. down he focused on me. Taking a deep breath I began. "I don't mean to dredge bad memories up but this concerns your murder".

Gabriel's stare became intense and I could tell this was a un-comfortable subject to be discussing so I just blurted it out to end it quickly. "I found the douche bags. They live just a few buildings over. Siliva actually found them because I had to be sneaky. I'm sorry but we have them. You can do something now to prove them guilty and put them away for a very long time. Gabriel's jaw started making little ticks and I could sense his anger. Bolting from the couch he roared down at me. "You fool of a girl, you can't go around interfering with the fates. You should have never done this".

Okay, that's definitely not the reaction I was hoping for. Tears crept from the corner of my eye's and I sobbed. "I'm sorry, I just wanted to do something for you and get the justice you deserve".

After a few moment's of silence something very unexpected happened , my guardian angel walked out on me. That's right, he tossed my window up and flew right out into the night sky. I waited around for his return but after two hours I started to worry. Was he gone for good? Did I screw up that bad? Was he just out cooling off like many couples do during a argument? I couldn't help but feel like I'd crossed the line but I truly thought I was doing a good deed. My heart was in my intentions and I never meant to hurt him or make him angry. Gosh, sometimes I can do the silliest things thinking I'm actually helping someone. Then another thought came to mind and my heart slammed into my ribcage. What if Gabriel went to seek them out himself and reap his revenge. That wouldn't be good for him. Grabbing my coat I headed to their home. If Gabriel was there I had to stop him from making a mistake. As I briskly walked the few meters it felt odd not having Gabriel by my side. His usual warmth was flowing around me and I wondered why we as humans never notice the tale-tale signs of another presence watching over us. Probably because we don't take time to smell the roses anymore. Life is one big rush these days, rush to work, rush to school, to practices. We spend more time on social media than with our family and friends. Rarely do people have conversations over coffee, now it's short abbreviated texts, and we spend way too much time arguing about who's opinion is right or who's opinion matters mores, when in reality everyone's opinion holds as much value as the next person's opinion even if you don't agree. Simply agree to disagree. Yes, we are so wrapped up in our wants and needs, so involved in ourselves we forget the beauty and good that's all around us. It's odd how it took an angel to finally open my eye's and wake me up, but my heart hurt knowing I had hurt my angel.

I slid inside the apartment building and was overwhelmed by the stinch of filth but I had to make sure Gabriel hadn't come here. After climbing three sets of stares I found the room I was looking for. Looking up and down the hall to make sure I was in the clear, I crept to the door. Ever so gently, I placed my ear to the door listening for any signs of a struggle. After few minutes I was satisfied at hearing nothing abnormal and turned to go. Turning around I came face to face with the monster myself, Gabriel's killer, Matt.

Gasping I tried to take off running but he clamped down on my arms and I could smell his vile breath heaving down on me. "What the fuck you doinf?"

Thinking quick, I tried to make up a plausible story. "Is this Shana's place? My boyfriend is cheating on me with that bitch. I was trying to hear and see if he was here".

Squinting his blood shot eye's at me he gave a slobbering grin. "That ain't no Shana's apartment girl. You got the wrong door. Matter of fact I've never heard of her and I know everybody in this building".

Trying to sound convincing I stated. "Well this is the address I was given by her ex boyfriend".

"Seems you been mislead girl. But don't worry, this may not have been a wasted trip after all. What you say me and you have alittle party?"

"No, I really must go now. Sorry to have bothered you". I tried to squeeze by him but he shoved me back into the wall and lifted the front of his shirt revealing a revolver. Fear seized my throat as I tried to come up with a solution. Grinning he revealed his rotting teeth and said. "We can do this the easy way or the hard way, your choice".

"This is my choice". I yelled and sailed the heel of my foot into his crotch. As he crumbled over I darted down the stairs but he was on me in no time. Clamping his sweaty hand over my mouth I bit down hard drawing blood. Whipping his gun out he shoved it into my skull and drug me down into the basement of the building. Once we stopped walking he shoved me down on the floor against the moldy wall. It was then that the reality of my situation kicked in and I started to cry. I knew this man was a cold hearted killer and I wouldn't make it out of here alive. Where was my angel was my only thought.

Chapter 14

Truth Unfolds

My head was reeling from the news Alisha just laid upon me. She may as well have dropped a nuclear bomb on me. Yes, I was angry at her even though her intentions were meant to be good. You just don't dig up someone's past, especially a past their trying to escape. Honestly my past hurt more than it angered me now. It's just a reminder of the stupid mistakes I made that cost me my life. Also I was scared, scared of what I may do if I ever found the coward that took my life as if I was nothing.

Things was going so great between Alisha and I, so I guess this is the storm before the calm. The realization dangling as a constant reminder that I'm dead, I'll never have Alisha. I never wanted love as a human, never felt the need to love another either, except the one time I made a mistake. Now that I'm no longer apart of this world I crave love, I've found true love, and I'm in love, only for it to be ripped away. The inevitable is destined to happen, I might as well get it over with. Alisha has turned her life around in the few short months that I've been here. I have absolute confidence that she will continue on the right path once I'm gone. Alisha knows this day is coming as well, we should both be prepared for it. Come tonight I will say my goodbyes and kiss my love one last time. I'm not doing this because I'm mad, no I'm doing this for her as well as myself. It's better to cut the ties now before we get in any deeper. I'll go back to her, tell her I'm leaving, hold her one more time and then tell her my truth. Tell her that I'm responsible for her father's death. Yes, I'm sure she'll hate me and I'll be doomed, but I deserve to be doomed. I deserve to suffer along with the memory of her love, along with the hurtful things I did when I was alive. Instead of using my wealth to help other's, I used it to weld control and power. While scoffing at the homeless man on the corner, I never worried where my next meal would come from. When seeing poor, hard working student's put everything they had into their studies, I was buying my grades. If only I could go back and make a difference I swear I'd be a better person, but sometimes you don't get second chances, or as in my case anyways.

I came to a stop when I realized where my ramblings had let me. I was outside of my luxury apartment that my parent's still maintained. The same apartment where I watched my life descend from my body. Stepping inside the scent of my choice cologne attacked my nose. Looking around my living room everything was as it should be, dust free, in place,. Top notch technology equipment, state of the arc furniture, suits tailored in Paris specifically for me. What was the point of owning such?

As I sat brooding I realized I wasn't mad at Alisha, but mad at myself. Mad that I took life for granted. What Alisha did for me was a gift. A gift to serve me justice, not hurt me. Feeling like a smuck, I left my old home in search of my new home on the ruddy side of town.

I couldn't wait to see her as I entered her tiny, yet cozy apartment. Everything was so her here and it enveloped me just as her hugs did. Noticing the apartment was empty I felt a twinge of uncertainty creep in. Had I hurt her so bad she seemed refuge at that slimy bar? Was she just out cooling down as I had done? Then a wadded piece of paper caught my eye. Unraveling it I saw that murdering bastards name and address scribbled on it. No, she wouldn't go there in search of me, would she? It's very possible considering the way I stormed out on her. Maybe she assumed I was out to seek my revenge. Throwing the window open I flew out at the speed of light. Within seconds I was at that building standing at his door. The scent of lavender, vanilla, and honey wafted in the air and I knew she had been here, that was Alisha's scent. Panic sat in as I searched the room for any trace of her. Oddly her scent was stronger in the hallway leading down the stairs. Using my instincts I hurled myself down the stairs and the scent grew stronger. It led me to a rusted door and I immediately entered where her scent overwhelmed me. I heard a distance muffled cry and took off in the direction of the sound. "What's your name bitch"? I heard that all to familiar voice snarl.

"Alisha Staley" she sobbed.

"Oh yea, your that girl who's old man offed himself. Yep I remember that. That dickhead of a bossman of his gave him the shaft and he couldn't handle it. Is it true you found him swinging in his closet?"

Alisha covered her ears and screamed "shut up, just shut up. You don't know anything about my dad. He was a good man".

Matt gave his rotton grin. "If it's any consolation, I snuffed that ass of a boss of his. Yep, Evan Carmichael' s not only fired your pop's, but he tried to steal my girl from me, so I had to shoot his ass dead".

"Evan's Carmichael". Alisha mumbled. I saw when she made the connection between me and Evan. Had I not taken her to my grave and shared my story with her she wouldn't have to find out like this. I watched as fresh tears erupted from her eye's. "Your lying. Evan wouldn't have fired my dad, not the Evan I know".

"Hate to break it to you doll face but he did. Google the shit".

"But Gabriel would have told me, he wouldn't have hid something like that from me".

Matthew gave her a strange look. "Look girl, I don't know what you been smoking and I don't know who the hell any Gabriel is or do I care. What I do know is your about to have the night of your life and just maybe if your good and do as I say I want kill you".

"Don't you dare come near me". Alisha screamed. Matt started to approach her while unbucklung his pants. So much rage filled me, anger for him exposing my darkest secret, anger at hurting Alisha, anger for having to see this scum once again. I was boiling mad. Before I could control my thoughts and anger I appeared but not just as the dark angel I normally was. No this time fire burned through my wings, my veins, my body. Matt's features froze on me and I heard Alisha whisper "Gabriel" fearfully. I slowly approached Matt as if I was a cat stalking a rat. "Remember me"? I asked and my voice came out like crackling fire as I bent down to his level giving him a good look. His body started to tremble and his lips twitched as he tried to speak through a dry mouth. "It's you. It can't be. I killed you, I watched you die".

Giving him a devilish smile I slowly shook my head no. "You made a bad mistake and a even bigger mistake by touching

Alisha. I know exactly where your going, I've seen it myself. You. Will. Rot."

"No, Cassidy made me do it. She begged me to kill you. I'm sorry, please have mercy".

"Did you bestow mercy upon me or your other victims? That's right, I know just how many lives you've ruined. I promise you will know what pain is everyday for eternity".

Placing my flaming hand around his throat I lifted him off the floor and held him above me. I watched as my fire burned him from the inside out. As he screamed flames licked up from inside his throat, poured from his eye's and nose. You could see the fire under his skin until he combusted into ash. It fell around us like confetti. My anger subsided as Alisha came to mind and my flames evaporated. I was now the normal Gabriel. Looking around I found Alisha huddled in a corner shivering from fear. Walking to her, I knelt down. "Let's get you home Alisha".

Shoving away from me she cried. "Stay away from me you monster. You killed my dad. Your a liar and just as bad as the guy you just killed".

Clearly Alisha was hysterical due to all the events combined, but I had no time to deal with her emotional distress at the moment. Ignoring her protests I swept her up into my embrace and flew us back to her apartment. Due to her emotions at the moment, I ran my hands over her eye's and put her to sleep. Once she woke rested, we would discuss her father and then I would take my leave. I could only hope for her forgiveness.

Chapter 15

Free Falling

The feeling that overcame me when I laid eye's on my killer was more than I could bare, but when I stood back and heard the things he said to Alisha and the vile things he had planned for her my emotions erupted like a volcano spewing lava. A power I never knew I possessed set my body aflame and i used it in ways I shouldn't have. It's not my decision to decide who lives and who dies but last night I took the matter into my own hands. Do I think he got what he deserved?..... absolutely. Did I do it for Alisha's protection?... of course. I knew once I returned I had A lot to answer for but I wasn't concerned at all. I was already doomed so how much worse could it get. I knew I was doomed because the look on Alisha's face when that dirtbag exposed my secret said it all. Then the words she threw at me, but I can't blame her. I hate myself too, probably more so.

I sat gazing at her sleeping form knowing that she would rise soon and the hard part was coming. Yes, it hurt having to leave her but it hurt more knowing she would hate me. Even though it turned my insides out I had to admit I hoped the best for her. I hoped she found true love again and he was more that I could ever be to her. I hoped she raised beautiful babies even if they wasn't mine. I wanted her to have the life she so deserved. I wished nothing but happiness for her. As I was in my feelings I saw her stir and swallowed hard. I knew the time was here and there was no amount of preparing that could make me ready enough. Slowly she sat up and as soon as her eye's landed on me tears started flowing. "I thought I told you to leave, get out". Alisha yelled clenching her blanket in her fists.

"Please Alisha, I know there's no amount of begging or pleading I can do to receive your forgiveness, but please hear me out. Let me explain".

'Whats to explain you ratchet person. Your responsible for making my dad feel like he was so worthless he didn't deserve to live. Your the reason I'm alone and living this condemned life."

Defensively I fired back as I zoomed into her face. "You don't think I know that. Trust me I do and I regret every minute of it. If I could change it I would. I live with it everyday"

Standing she jabbed her finger into her chest. "And I don't? When I think of my dad now all I see is him hanging by his fucking belt in his closet. Now, not only when I think of that gruesome scene, I'll think of the man I loved was responsible for making him feel he had no other choice. The man I loved is the reason my life is so fucked up."

My body froze at her admittance. Never had we told each other of our feelings. Never had we uttered words about love or devotion. I loved Alisha so hard, so complete, but I never told her because I knew I had to leave. Now she tells me under these circumstances and I had to wonder what she meant when she said "the man I loved". Did she no longer love me? Did the truth douse the flame on her love for me? I had to know. "You said you loved me Alisha"?

"Yes I did, but that was before this bomb exploded. I can't love the person who caused me so much pain, who hid behind a disguise knowing what they caused my family. What I felt for you is gone, no more. I can barely stand the sight of you now".

Gripping her arms I pleaded. "Don't say that Alisha. I love you and always will. There's nothing I can do to change the past. You don't know how bad I wish I could. If I could bring your dad back I'd do it in a heartbeat. All I want for you is to be happy, to continue with all your plans and dreams you had before this travesty. I understand you don't love me, I don't blame you, I hate myself too, but please let's not part ways like this. I have to go back now and I can't bare leaving knowing that I broke you, hurt you, knowing you hate me. I'm begging for your forgiveness". I sank to my knees in front of her, my wings tucked behind my back, my hands cupping her fragile hands, and my head resting upon our hands. "Please Alisha" I whispered horsely.

Giving me a cold glare she spoke in a venom laced voice. "What would make me happy is your disappearance for good".

My heart cracked in half then shattered into a million different pieces. I could feel the fragments scratching the inside of my chest. Whoever said angels didn't cry was a lie. I was crying for the first time in my life. Standing on shaky legs I looked down at her. Bending down, I placed a long, gentle kiss to her forehead and pulled her tightly into me. Wrapping my wings around her along with my arms I whispered. "If only I could have found you in my Human life, how I would have loved you, how things would be so different. I wish nothing but the best for you and follow those dreams." With one last tight squeeze I looked into her crystal orbs and vanished.

Chapter 16

Time Heals All Wounds

As I watched Gabriel disappear from my life forever, I collapsed to the floor in a heap of tears. I wasn't crying because he was gone, no I was crying for all the hurt and anger I've kept bottled up over the years. The loss of my dad, the reckless path I had chosen, the love I had given to the one who was responsible for my dad's suicide. I don't know how long I laid on that wooden floor but forever still wouldn't have given me enough time to cry all my hurt away. Pulling myself to my feet a sudden urge to be destructive came over me. I desperately wanted a taste of liqueur and any drug available, but I was determined to fight that urge. Spotting a glass vase I picked it up and hurled it against the wall smashing it into a million pieces. Next, I moved on to glasses, dishes, anything that was breakable. By the time I was done it looked as if a bull had rampaged a China shop. Still not satisfied but refusing to give in to those urges that would bring complete numbness and run to the closest bar I picked up a notepad and pen and begin writing. I wrote down all my anger, sadness, hopes, unleashing abuse on the pad and pen. I wrote until there was no more ink or paper, until my fingers cramped. Crashing onto my bed I cried myself to sleep.

In the morning I was woken by my alarm blareing tunes from my favorite pop station I listened to as a teen. Confused, I sat up slowly and was dumbfounded. I was in my childhood room surrounded by my bright, flowerdy comforter, with my school awards hanging all over my wall. Panic spliced through me as I fumbled from the bed. Noticing I was dressed in my Hello Kitty pajamas, I ran my hand over my body and noticed I was thinner and my boobs smaller. Racing to my dresser mirror I gazed at my reflection. Gone was the crazy dyed hair, gone was the faint crinkles near my eye's caused from stress, drugs, and late night drinking. Taking a seat right there on my floor tears sprung from my eye's as I realized this had all been one terribly long nightmare that I could vaguely remember. I remember my dad's suicide, finding him, going wild partying, sex with stranger's, and this mysterious angel with a gorgeous set of black wing's that I couldn't keep my hands off of. Oddly though, I couldn't recall his name or face even though we made love, he flew me to the Golden Gate Bridge, he turned to fire and killed some man that wanted to harm me. I couldn't recall him, but I could remember certain things he did and that he was sent to me to save my soul, and strangely just the thought of him made butterflies scatter in my stomach and warmth flood my cheeks. Almost felt like I loved him. Why couldn't I see his face though or at least remember a name. Taking a deep breath I mumbled. "What a strange, horrific dream Alisha. No more scary movies for you".

Hearing dishes clatter in the kitchen I bolted out my door and scurried down the hall. There my dad stood over the stove preparing my breakfast as he did every morning. I stood there taking him in as images of his death played in my mind. Get a grip, I mentally told myself. It was just a vivid dream, nothing more. My eye's swelled with tears as I watched my dad hop around the kitchen. Finally he noticed me standing there and stopped. Taking me in he asked. "Are you okay pumpkin?"

Nodding my head yes, I launched myself into his arms hugging him tight while inhaling his soapy scent. "I'm fine dad. I just had a terrible dream and it seemed so real".

"Care to talk about?"

Shaking my head no, I said. "I just want to forget about it dad"

Pulling away, he felt my forehead and mumbled. "You don't feel feverish pumpkin but you do look rather under the weather. Why don't you stay home from school today and rest up".

That seemed like a fabulous idea. Normally I would've protested since I've only missed three days of school my entire life. Once for having my tonsils removed at eight, then at ten I fell off my bike and broke my arm, and at thirteen when I got my period for the first time. Today I honestly felt drained and I'd never had a dream to shake me so. "I think I will dad".

We sat down for breakfast and made small talk as we ate. Finally my dad was off to work and I hugged him bye wishing him a good day and to be careful. After his departure I looked around the house as if I hadn't seen it in years, and it really felt like it. Trying to ease my mind, I cranked up the outdated stero and washed up the breakfast dishes. I remembered my eighteenth birthday was coming up in a few weeks and dad always went out of his way to make my birthdays extra special. I don't know why but I felt extra grateful for all my dad does for me, I guess the fear of losing him in the dream got me to thinking.

Okay enough about that dream already and that sexy dark angel too. To busy myself I grabbed my school books to do some studying. I know, who studies on a day off, right? I do. My grades are my only hopes of getting me and my dad out of here, besides I'm not one of the pretty girls therefore I have zero of a social life and a non-existent love life. As a matter of fact I've never been kissed. I'm not a prude by no means, it's just guys aren't into me. I have stringy blonde hair, narrow hips and I've seen thirteen year old's with more boobs than me. So yea, I'm not really a catch. Dad teases me and claims I'm a late bloomer. Man, I wished I had the body I had in my dream. My hips were rounder, my boobs brag worthy, and I wasn't this shy little meek mouse that I am now. I could only hope that by my twenties I'm rocking my dream body. And there he was again, my dark angel smothering me in a kiss, crawling between my legs. "Ugh, stop it" I scolded myself. Never has a dream worked me up so bad. Then I remembered something from the dream. I remembered leaving a store and almost smashing my fingers in the door, yet the door would stop before slamming my fingers. Five percent curious and ninety-five percent stupidy, I walked to my bedroom door. I laid my fingers on the frame and taking a deep breath, I gave the door a good swing. "Ahhhhhhhh... son of a biscuit".

Quickly I pulled my fingers free and rubbed them. By the time I made it to the kitchen to grab a bag of frozen peas they was bruising and starting to swell. Laughing at myself I knew beyond a shadow of a doubt that my dream was just that..... a dream.

Chapter 17

Broken Wings

Leaving Alisha behind during such a messy time was by far the hardest thing I've ever done, even harder than facing down my killer. To make matters worse, I had torn her heart apart and knowing I was the cause of her pain was like hot pokers scorching my skin. I never meant for any of these to happen. I never meant to fall in love with her and hearing her utter those last words to me is by far more torturing than anything my doom has planned for me. I constantly heard her voice echo in my head "I hate you, leave, get out". Yes, I'm suffering more than anything can bring down upon me. I simply didn't care what awaited me on the other side. Maybe it Will hurt bad enough to make me forget Alisha.

Upon entering my newfound kingdom all the other angels turned away from me. I suppose I was being shunned because I failed my mission, because my soul was doomed for eternity. Not caring I walked on through the hall of angels determined to meet my maker and get this over with. As I was almost at the end, Belle floated down from out of no where. "Follow me Gabriel".

With heavy shoulders, I asked no questions but followed in behind her. Soon we appeared in a very lovely garden. Flowers I had never seen before bloomed so vibrantly. A stream of the clearest water trickled ever so pleasantly over the rarest stones known to man. In the trees bird's chirped a beautiful tune and the grass was greener than any other. Paradise was the only word for it. Suddenly a very bright golden light descended from above. So bright I had to shield my eye's. Peering through the brightness, my eye's beheld such a sight. Another male angel floated down to us, his light dimming. He was very large, at least stood near eight feet tall. Bell's voice interrupted my thoughts. "This is Artimis. He is the first messenger and will speak to you now".

Belle said no more before she disappeared leaving me with this mammoth of a man. Leveling his gaze on me, I stood as erect as I could ready to accept whatever wrath he laid upon me with dignity. He finally spoke and when he did his voice rumbled. "Gabriel?"

"Yes". I spoke clearly.

"You have passed the test".

Test, I thought confused. "Forgive me, I don't understand".

"Gabriel, you was brought here under unfair circumstances, yet you lived you life on the careless side. You was sent back to earth to save another humans soul but not just any human. You was purposely sent to save a human that you unintentionally caused harm to, enough that her life took another course. That human was Alisha Staley. We've watched Alisha flourish under your care and change her destiny. However, you broke many boundaries with this Alisha. I want go into details, but I'm sure you realize what you did".

I hung my head to show my shame as he continued in that rumbling voice. "Your love for her can be sensed as well as her love for you. We have chosen to give you another chance but this time as a human again. You will return back to earth once again as Evan Carmichael and resume your life where you left off. You will remember everything from your time here as well as what brought you here, however, Alisha will not know you or recall much of anything. She will wake to think it was all a dream. Her father will still be alive and she seventeen. Before I send you off beware, this is your final chance so please choose wisely, for your choices will lead to your fate".

Looking up at him in awe I started to speak but I was sent into a swirling motion and I was tumbling down a tunnel of golden light and that's all I can recall. I woke up naked on my bed to the bright morning sun. Sitting up slowly I glanced around my apartment and as I rose I felt lighter. My wings were gone along with the extra weight they placed on me. Turning to see my back in the mirror, I was greeted by two long scars on each shoulder blade, evidence of where my wings had been. Looking at the clock I realized I had two hours before I reported to work. Racing to my fridge, I grabbed the juice and chugged it down. How I had missed the simple taste of food. So many things I had overlooked and taken for granted, but not this time around. I would be a better person and make a difference. After a shower I headed to work and when I spotted my dad I ran over hugging him, remembering his tormented face at having learned of my death. "What's gotton into you son?" He laughed.

"Isn't it just a glorious day dad. I'm just happy to be alive".

Chucking he swayed his hand as a indication to get to work. Skipping to my office I made sure to joyfully greet everyone I passed. This gained me a lot of strange looks, seeing how my old self was a grump. Taking a seat behind my desk I saw my paperwork just as I had left it except Mr. Staley's name stood out. Yes, I still get to chat with him. I had to get near Alisha. Yes, I was twenty-four and her almost eighteen, but she was my one even if she didn't know it and her dad was my ticket. Buzzing his supervisor I asked for Mr. Staley to be sent back. Moments later there was a knock on my door. "Enter" I called. As Mr. Staley entered I rose with a smile and extended my hand. "Pleasure to meet you Mr. Staley. I've heard great things about you. "

"You have?" He asked somewhat surprised.

Quick to cover my mistake I nodded. "Of course. Now what was it you wished to discuss?"

Mr. Staley went on to explain the safety measures that needed to be taken care of and how if we were randomly inspected we could be fined. Nodded my head I agreed. "Thanks Mr. Staley for bringing this to my attention. I will see to it right away and have the equipment ordered".

A look of shock crossed his face. Man, I must have really been a rotton boss as well as person. Clearing my throat I went on to ask. "How long have you been with the company Mr. Staley?"

Knitting his brows together he answered. "Almost twenty year's Sir"

"Please, call me Ga-Evan. That's dedication there. A lot of hours spent here. When was your last raise?"

"Sir.. Evan, I've never had one".

"Hmmmm.... what is your pay now?"

"Eleven a hour, Sir".

Nodding my head I spoke. "Expect a pay increase on your next check Mr. Staley".

The joy that crossed his face made me feel very good. He was beaming and I was thrilled. Who knew it felt this good to be giving and understanding. Standing he thanked me and shook my hand. As he made his departure I stopped him. "Didn't you mention that your daughter had a birthday coming up?"

Taking a moment to think he said. "I may have. Yes, it's next Thursday".

"Take that day off with pay and do something special for her, okay?"

"Yes, most definitely Sir. Thank you so much".

Once he left I got busy getting to know my employees and deciding where to give raises. Not only that I had a plan to see Alisha. It was time to have our first company picnic where the employees could bring there families. I will have my Alisha.

Chapter 18

Parties And Picnics

Running around the kitchen, I was rummaging for a spatula in hopes of rescuing the chicken from burning. What can I say, cooking is not one of my talents. I'm strictly a right out of the can and straight to the microwave kinda girl. I figured since I'd bummed at home all day I'd take the burden of cooking off of my dad for the night. The table was almost set when my dad walked through the door with a bounce in his step. Spotting my charred chicken, lumpy smashed potatoes, and overcooked carrots he smiled. "Smells wonderful sweetie".

"Okay dad, it's fine, you don't need to lie". He grinned and placed a kiss atop my head. I noticed he seemed overly happy. "What's the deal with you?"

Taking a seat, he piled his plate with my less than spectacular food. "You want believe what happened today".

"Ummmm..... You finally asked Janet out on a date?" I said hopeful. Janet was his co-worker and just happened to be divorced. The chemistry was so obvious between the two, yet they both danced around the topic of hooking up. Plus both were too scared to get involved. My dad stared at me over the rim of his glasses. "No,Alisha. And I'm not about to discuss my romantic life with you".

"You mean lack of romantic life dad".

"Alisha". He warned.

"What? I'm just saying dad, you can't keep locked away from the world. You deserve to have a life beyond me and work".

"Are you finished Alisha?"

"I guess".

"Good. Now here's for the good news. My boss approved my ideas".

"That's great dad".

"That's not all baby, he also gave me a raise".

"What? That is the best news we've heard in a long time. Wait I thought you said this new, young boss was bull headed..... hmmmm..... maybe he got laid".

"Alisha". My dad hissed. "Language please".

Snickering we dug into this roadkill meal I had made.

My eighteenth birthday arrived and my dad was actually given the day off. We made the best of it too. My dad insisted on splurging on me since he received the raise. Taking me to the mall he allowed me to pick out a new outfit complete with shoes. Afterwards he took me to eat sushi, which was a first for both of us. Usually we didn't have the money to spend like this, but dad insisted this day be special. Once home we attacked the homemade cake dad made for me every year, strawberry and cream, my absolute favorite.

A few weeks passed and I found myself riding along in my dad's bucket of rust of a car. His company was having a family oriented picnic. Naturally I dreaded this, I was so not a people person but this was important to dad, relunticaly I agreed to go. I slid into my new outfit and shoes, brushed my untameable hair, and applied a smidgen of mascara along with a pale pink lipstick. Rushing out the door, I gave my cheeks a good pinch for that natural glow. At least this picnic was at a favorite park of mine where I knew of a abandoned, old church down a beaten path I could escape to if it became to much. Getting out of the car I followed my dad on over. We stopped several times to make small talk with a few of his fellow coworkers. Finally we made it to the food table and the spread was made from heaven. All my favs were in plain view awaiting for me to devour them. It was certain that I would leave this picnic not being able to walk from food overload. Grabbing a plate, I filled it to the brim with all these delightful foods. We had just sat down and I had my fork fisted preparing to make a pig of myself when I heard a kinda of familiar voice. "Hello there, Mr. Staley".

My dad looked up from his plate and smiled. "Hi Mr. Carmichael".

"Please, call me Evan".

This Evan stared into my eye's as if he was reading my soul. Suddenly filled with embarrassment over my two-ton plate, I gently laid my fork aside. Evan was a walking dream and I looked like Miss Piggy in the middle of a food orgy. The ground would do me a grave favorite right now if it just open up and swallow me whole. My dad's voice scattered my thoughts as he said. "Allow me to introduce you to my daughter, Alisha".

Remembering my manners, I gave a shy smile and extended my hand. Evan's much larger hand engulfed mine and a tremor of warmth surpassed me. This man was such a hottie, heat eradicated from him, or my imagination was just running wild. "Alisha, this is my boss". My dad continued, but I might as well have been deaf. Still gripping my hand Evan smiled showing off a perfect smile. Then I noticed I had whipped icing slathered on my hand from a cookie I had nibbled on while walking to the table. Now that icing was clambered on his hand as well. Jerking my hand away, I gasped. "I'm so sorry. I didn't me to get my cream on you". Rushing my hand to cover my mouth at how that sounded, my cheeks flared as I prayed for a storm to miraculously appear and lightening strike me down. "That's not what I meant, I, um, let me wash you. I mean wash your hand". OMG Alisha just shut up, I screamed to myself. Thank Jesus my dad's attention had been averted into a another coworkers conversation and he didn't hear this somewhat inappropriate conversation. Taking a deep breath, I pronounced my words carefully to make sure nothing came out sounded like sex addict. "Please, let me get you a napkin".

Giving me a sexy smile he lowered his eye's and slowly licked the cream from his hand. "I happen to love cream".

Wait, what. Did I just witness this Goddess of a man lick cream off his hand. Not any cream but cream that had been on my hand. Then say what he said in a dark, sensual voice that caused my thighs to clamp together. No, this can't be right. I'm only eighteen and he's like got to be in his twenties, not to mention my dad's boss. Plus men like him just don't flirt with me. If I was bold, I would assume he was lost, over here flirting with me.

Giving me a knowing smile he placed his fingers under my chin and said with a wink. "I'll be seeing you Alisha".

What the fuck just happened? Things like that just don't happen to me. Once he was out of view I attacked my plate clearly eating my emotions. As the day wore on, every time I glanced around I found Evan's eye's on me, watching my every move. After a bit I wondered back over to the food table. Grabbing a napkin, I picked a assortment of cookies and headed down my hidden path for a bit of downtime. No longer than it took me to gobble up my first cookie I heard his voice. "Fancy seeing you here?"

"Oh". Was all I could manage to say as I brushed cookie crumbs from my mouth and shirt. I was literally caught with my hand in the cookie jar, shoveling them in my mouth faster than a fat kid at a candy bar. Why must I keep humiliating myself in front of this man. "This is a very beautiful place, isn't it?"

Nodding my head, I agreed. "It is. So peaceful. I wasn't aware anyone else knew about it?"

Taking a seat beside me he spoke. "A very special person showed this place to me. I come here often now".

"Oh". Gosh I sounded like a idiot. Honestly I didn't know what to say and as I checked out his side profile I gasped. A flashback came to me. I knew his face I just couldn't recall where. Looking over at me he asked. "Something wrong?".

"Um, I, um. Have we ever met before? I mean your voice sounds familiar and you face?"

Giving me that grin he stood and trailed his thumb over my lip swiping off some crumbs I had missed. "I don't know Alisha. You tell me".

What the hell was that suppose to mean, but the sensation his thumb imprinted on my lip invaded any thoughts. Staring absentmindily, he took my hand and pulled me up. "We should head back before your dad starts to worry".

Evan took a step and the sunlight shone in through a hole in the roof. For a hair of a second his body was lit up in a bright, shiny glow and another memory hit me full force. Taking a few steps from me, I recalled the angel in that nightmare a few weeks ago. The dream I had put behind me. "What's wrong?" He asked taking a step toward me.

"I, I must go". I left him there as I ran out of the church with my mind in a whirlwind. Thankfully my dad was ready to leave once I returned. I stayed up late that night snacking on some of my favorite things my dad brought home from the picnic. Between fistfulls of sweets and thinking of that dream and Evan's confusing attention I was worse for wear in the morning.

Chapter 19

High Above Me

S o may be I came on a bit strong at my first meeting with Alisha, but I was overwhelmed at seeing her. What I really wanted to do was whisk her off and tell her we were meant to be, made for each other. However, I knew I had to take things slow with her. This wasn't the same Alisha I knew. No, this younger Alisha wasn't like the bad attitude tough girl I knew. This Alisha was delicate, skittish, and not jaded by the cruel world yet. She wore her heart on her sleeve, and innocence poured from her like a fountain. Clearly she was still untouched by a man judging by that sweet blush that crept over her cheeks at my nearness and her bumbling words. Just me flirting with her sent her scurrying off like a scared mouse. I know she's only eighteen and I twenty-four, but I have to make her mine. She must remember on her own terms.

Before she rushed from that rotting church it seemed some form of recognition entered her brain. All I want to do is hold her in my arms and keep her safe, assure her that nothing will ever hurt her and make her life better. My next move was devising another plan to get near her without her dad thinking I'm some kinda weirdo.

As I sat atop a bridge, bad habits are hard to break. Yes, I still seek out high places even though I have to climb now, to do my thinking. That's when it came to me. I recall her father saying once that she had to walk home from school and worried about the weather. That's it, tomorrow I will wait for school to be released and offer her a ride. Yes it's risky and I need to be careful because I don't want to scare her off, but I've got to see her. Luckily I'm the boss so I can come and go as I please.

The following evening I waited down the road from the school for her to stroll by. Finally I spotted my little angel walking hurriedly along by herself. She tried to sheild herself from the cold winds while balancing her books. Whipping my Porsche to the curb I rolled the window down and called to her. "Alisha, hey Alisha"

Slowly she peeked over her shoulder but kept walking. Obviously she didn't recognize me. Tooting my horn she finally stopped and peered through the window. "Hi Alisha, you remember me?"

Shyly she shrugged. "Your Mr. Carmichael, my dad's boss".

"Yep, and call me Evan. I'm too old to be addressed as a Mr. So, where you heading?"

"Home actually".

"Well hop in, I'll give you a ride"

Looking uncertain, she mumbled. "I don't think that's a good idea. I can really walk home, it's no problem"

"I insist Alisha. It's cool out and to be honest I'd feel like shit if I allowed you to walk home in this weather".

Please bite on that story I silently prayed. Giving a nervous glance around she slowly reached for the door handle and slid in. "I guess it's okay this one time. I hate putting you out of your way though".

Oh my goodness, could she get any sweeter I gushed. "Seriously baby, I don't mind at all".

Turning the heat up to get her warm I pulled away from the curb. "You really have a nice car Evan".

Oh, hearing my name slide between her lips was like melted butter. Smiling toward her I replied. "Thank you baby, but having nice things isn't what life is all about".

And there she was, my old Alisha. I saw her eye's roll at my words and a slight snort escaped her. "Says the person who doesn't have to worry financially".

Immediately she covered her mouth and her cheeks were stained pink as I laughed. "I'm so sorry Evan, I didn't mean it like it sounded".

It's ok buttercup. You didn't hurt my feelings any. Actually your very right, those that don't know the struggle don't know the pain. Please always say what you feel to me. I won't get upset".

"Okay then Evan. This is what's bothering me, is this appropriate, me accepting a ride from my dad's boss?"

"I don't see any problems in giving a beautiful girl a ride". I tried to hide the snicker in my voice at my choice of words and it was clear Alisha grasped what I said as well due to her bright cheeks. Clearing my throat I spoke in a more serious tone. "Truth is Alisha, I'm planning on opening a soup kitchen and I'm looking for recruits. Would you be interested?"

Truth was I just came up with that from off the top of my head. I had no plans to do no such of a thing, but our conversation about struggles lit a lightbulb in my head. Besides it will allow me to see her without sitting outside of her school like a stalker.

Eventually she noticed I was headed to the upper side of town when she asked concerned. "Where are you going? I don't live on this side of town".

"Yes, I know, but I'm hungry and could really use some company while I eat. Plus we can discuss ideas for the kitchen"

Glancing down at her clothes she said. "I'm not dressed for the restaurants on this side of town and I really need to get home. I have chores and homework to see to".

"Don't worry buttercup, I think you look wonderful and I promise I'll have you home in time to do your chores".

I know I was probably coming off as kidnapper but I had to make her remember, I had to be near her. Just having her sit beside me in my car was driving me insane. Finally we arrived at the restaurant and I ordered for both of us. "I hope you like beef Wellington?"

Shrugging and giving a half smile she said. "Never heard of it"

"You'll love it, trust me".

I started making small talk at first. Asking about school, her goals, college interests and such, then I decided to take the conversation deeper. "Do you believe in the supernatural".

Quirking her eyebrows in question she asked. "Like?"

"You know, monsters, special powers, you know maybe angels?"

"Hmmmm..... Not much. I mean there was this..... oh never-mind. It was just a crazy dream and...."

Alisha's voice trailed off leaving me in wonder. I knew by her deep expression she recalled something but was hiding it. "Oh come on do share?" I tried to goad her.

"No, it's very strange and I don't won't to come off as crazy, plus I don't know you well enough to share this".

Oh if you only knew how well you know me Alisha, I thought. "Please"? I tried to sound pitiful. "Tell ya what, you tell me you can ask me whatever you like and I have to answer".

"Fine Evan, but don't judge me".

"Never Alisha".

"Okay, have you ever had a dream so vivid it seemed real, that has you sccond guessing if it really happened?"

I listened intently as she told the story of us. I so badly wanted to fill in on certain parts, especially our ending, but I kept my trap shut.

"And that's it, but the strange thing is I can't recall for the life of me what he looked like or his name no matter how hard I try".

She stared down into her empty plate as if she was lost in thoughts. It was obvious this really got to her. Before I could say anything she spoke again. "You know there's places here that draw me to them and I can't explain why. Once I go I can remember me being there with my angel but still no clues. That old church was one of those and for a instant.... oh nevermind. It was just my imagination. And when I see the Golden Gate Bridge a warm feeling comes over me, like some sort of connection. You think I'm crazy now?"

"Not at all. I understand .."

Before I could complete my sentence she gasped. "Oh no, the time. I've got to get home".

Once at the car she went to open the door and it started to close on her fingers. Fast as could be I caught the door before her fingers could be damaged. Alisha stood there like stone, almost comatose. "Gabriel" she whispered. My breath caught in my chest at her words. A bright, loving smile creased her face as she looked up at me. "Gabriel was his name".

Remember baby please I silently begged. "He was mine. His name was Gabriel. I still can't see his face though."

I tucked her safely into my car and drove her home.

Chapter 20

Mixed Emotions

Okay, so this was like so awkward, I mean imagine a girl like me stealing the attention from a man like Evan. For the life of me I couldn't figure out his intentions. Was he hitting on me or was he just being nice to some poor kid? Whatever the reason was I loved the attention. Who wouldn't love it, I mean Evan is super sexy and to die for. He made me feel things I shouldn't be feeling toward him, after all he is my dad's boss so this could get messy. Who am I kidding? Evan picked me up from school once, fed me, and wants me to work along beside him on a feed the needy project, that doesn't mean he likes me. I must stop reading into this. Evan's a grown, successful man, I'm barely out of high school and have boobs the size of tic-tacs, and my looks are less than steller. I've never attracted the attention of the male species and I'm not exactly Miss socialite.

Not to mention Evan probably thinks I'm some type of lunatic after I shared my dream with him earlier this evening. God, I can't believe I shared that with him but this strange calming effect comes over me when I'm with him. I can't truly describe it but it's like I'm put at ease, but enough about that because the last few weeks have been even stranger in a good yet creepy kind of way. Almost a week after I last saw Evan another odd vision popped into my head. I kept seeing a headstone by a tree in the cemetery uptown. I couldn't make out the word's etched onto the stone but I knew if I didn't go in search my mind wouldn't rest. The next day I hopped the bus to uptown and made my way to the cemetery. The sun hadn't quite sat yet so there was a rosy gold tint to the Fall sky. After walking around aimlessly for a bit I finally spotted the tree in my vision. Rushing over I searched the area but there's was no such stone. Berating myself for being so silly I turned to go and ran smack dab into a hard chest. I started to fall back but strong arms wrapped around my waist breaking my fall. Righting myself, I saw that it was Evan. To stunned to speak I just stood there gaping at him. Evan grinned down at me. "Fancy seeing you here Alisha".

"Oh, I, ummm".

"Shhh...theres no need to explain. I understand. I too come here often".

"You do?"

"Yes. I have family here".

"Oh right".

"So, what brings you here?"

"Oh nothing. Just walking".

Evan looked at me as if he knew the truth then smiled while placing his arm over my shoulders to lead me away. I don't know Why but being tucked under his arm felt so familiar and right. Almost if this wasn't the first time. Working up the nerve I placed my arm around his back as we walked. Slowly I rubbed my hand up and down and felt a odd bumpy feeling. "What is that Evan?"

Evan froze and looked at me. I sensed the tension rolling off him. "I'm sorry. I shouldn't have asked."

Snapping out of it, Evan whispered. "No, it's okay. It's scars I received. Scars that taught me a life lesson as well as changed my life. They remind me of the person I can be. I'm actually very proud of them."

Before I knew it Evan was stripping his shirt from his body. It was hard not to keep my eyes from roaming his delectable body as I watched his muscles ripple against his movements. Once his shirt was off he turned giving me a full view of his back. There, on both sides of his back was two long twin scars. Naturally I wondered the cause but didn't want to ask. Slowly I held my hand out and lightly connected my finger to one of them. Softly I trailed the length and as I did a vision hit me like a bolt of lightening. I saw black angel wings. The same wings as my angel, as Gabriel. Starting to tremble I placed my other hand on the opposite scar and was attacked with another vision. Gabriel... I could see Gabriel's face vividly. Then I'd see Evan's face until the two meshed together as one. Then the tombstone writings popped into my head with Evan's name. Gasping, I dropped my hands and stepped back. Evan turned to face me. "Gabriel" I croaked.

Evan's eyes seemed to gloss over with moisture. "Yes Alisha".

This was way to much to handle and I fled with Evan on my heels. I could hear him calling my name and begging me to stop. Finally he caught me around the waist and sent us both tumbling to the ground. Of course he landed on top of me. "What are you?" I screamed through a sob.

"I'm human again Alisha. You saved me. You did it. I've been praying for you to figure this out. I missed you so much"

"This can't be. It was just a wacko dream, nothing more. Your not real. Your just some crazy playing on my emotions. What do you want from me?"

"You know what I want Alisha. I want you. Your dad's back safe and sound and I'm here for my second chance at life as well as with you".

"Let me go now".

"Kiss me Alisha, kiss me".

"Never. Your crazy. Things like this don't happen"

"Let me take you back to my place and make love to you again over and over. Let's be what we once was, even better. Please, I can't give you everything".

I finally opened my eye's and looked into his eye's. I knew instantly that he was my Gabriel. No other had those kind, gentle eye's. Placing my hand against his Cheek I whispered "Gabriel".

"Yes baby, it's me. We can get married tomorrow. You can leave your life forever".

"No Gabriel. This is too much. I'm confused, scared, and only in high school. Please let me up. Let me go home".

"Your killing me Alisha. I need you now". He started kissing my neck and rocked his hips into mine. "Please Gabriel, no, I'm scared".

Giving a deep breath he sat up. "Fine. I'll take you home but know this, I'll never let you go".

Chapter 21

Get A Grip

What in the hell just happened. One minute I was just standing there and the next I found myself on the ground with Gabriel, Evan, or whatever his name is on top of me. Not only did he have me pinned down, but he was sucking on my neck, grinding his hardness into me through our clothes and speaking of marriage. All I could think was shit dude, I just discovered my dream was in fact real and I wasn't going insane and you want to lay it on me like that. Seriously just back off will ya. Give me a chance to digest this madness and come to terms with this revelation.

Okay, fine, I admit I would have probably allowed Gabriel to devour me right there had it not been for the turmoil in my mind. I mean he's hot and technically we have had sex. Not just bland, vanilla sex, but flipping me over, pulling hair, biting, spanking my ass type of sex. But that was before, when my life was upside down. When he came to me in order to save my soul, and that he did. Not only did he save my soul but he brought my dad back as well as was given another chance himself. Now that I know that Evan is actually Gabriel so many more visions are coming to me. Tender moment's we shared, I was a tattoo artist which seems laughable now. I recall why Gabriel was murdered and me getting kidnapped by said murderer, only to have Gabriel come to my rescue. But things are different now, I mean yea, I loved Gabriel to no end before I discovered he was responsible for my dad's suicide. Now, so much was different. True, I still loved Gabriel but Evan seems different from the Gabriel I knew. Could I possibly love Evan as I do Gabriel. Yes, they are technically the same person, but I was a different version of myself while I was with Gabriel. I wasn't this shy, naive, high school virgin that I am now. No bad ass Alisha was fierce, strong, very opinated, and took no shit. Could I find her again? Or better yet, do I want to. Honestly i couldn't imagine myself ever being that Alisha, and once Evan finds out I'm not the Alisha he fell for would he still want me?

Gosh, all these unanswered questions had my head spinning and I was on the verge of a panic attack. The car ride home was a strain as well. We rode in thick silence, both lost in our own thoughts. The last words he spoke to me was haunting, "no matter what, you will be mine". Really? What's that suppose to mean? Was it a threat? A promise? Or just mindless chatter?

Times like this I wish I really had a friend to confide in. Usually I told my dad everything but not this, no way, no how. I could see it now.... oh, by the way dad, your boss and I go way back, yep, he's responsible for you whacking yourself but your back now. I'm sure my dad would be thrilled... not.

Strange thing is I do want Evan in this strange, school girl fantasy way. I mean I'm a geek, I'm talking major loser here. Then some hot, older, rich guy wants me, Alisha Staley. It's like pretty woman minus all the hooker stuff. Hell I've never been kissed let alone pawed by a boy. Quick reminder, Evan was a boy, Evan was a man, a fine looking man at that. A smile crept to my face and I new beyond a reasonable doubt that I too wanted Evan. Making up my mind I decided it was worth a shot and finally let sleep come.

The next morning I woke and rushed through my shower. Today was the day, I was going to approach Evan just like the other Alisha would do. I took extra time on my appearance and left the house earlier than my norm. I gave my dad the excuse of a early study hall to keep him from questioning me further. Catching the bus uptown I knew exactly where to go. I remembered where Evan said he lived. The building was beautiful and smelled of money. Within no time I was standing in front of his door. Taking a deep breath and with shaky hands, I buzzed. The wait seemed to take forever and I was on the verge of sprinting off when the door opened. Evan grinned confidently when he saw me. That cocky smuck, I thought. Not waiting for his invite, I put on the best cocky attitude I could muster and pushed my way inside his pad. Chuckling at my abruptness, Evan said. "Sure, come on in Alisha. What do I owe to this pleasure".

Swirling around to face him with my hands on my hips I snorted. "Cut the shit Gabriel. We need to talk and set some boundaries".

Placing his finger on his chin he took a second to ponder what I said. "Hmmm... I'm not to fond of boundaries Alisha".

"Tough bad boy. Now you are or else I'll walk out that door and scream bloody murder if you ever come near me".

"Okay, fine. You practically have me by the balls now Alisha. Let's hear your boundaries"

Lifting my chin over winning my first victory I stared him in the eye with all seriousness. "First, I'm sure you already know that I am a virgin. I haven't experienced half of what the other Alisha has done. I've never drank, partied, or been kissed for that matter".

Giving a sly Grimm he started moving toward me. "We can fix some of that right now".

Clenching my fists, I gritted out. "Boundaries Gabriel, boundaries".

Holding his hands up in surrender he sighed. "Fine Alisha, I get it. I'll give you your stupid boundaries. I'll do whatever it takes to get us back to where we were. Now how about a kiss?"

"What" I screeched. "Did you not just here anything I said Gabriel?"

"Oh for Christ sake Alisha, it's just a innocent kiss. It's not like I'm popping your cherry".

"M-my what?" I stuttered.

A blank expression crossed his face. "You know Alisha that thin line of sk..."

Gasping I shrieked. "I know what the hell it is, I just can't believe you said that".

Smirking he rattled on. "Wooo... I'm glad you do. I thought for a minute there I was going to have to talk to you about the birds and the bees".

"Your such a cunt Gabriel".

Laughing he said. "One little kiss Alisha. That's all. Just let me taste those lips. It's been too long".

Yes, it had been too long and I admit I was curious as well. "Fine, but nothing more".

"Promise I'll only kiss you Alisha".

Walking over to me he pulled me to him and looked down into my face. Nervously I licked my lips. "It's a honor to be your first kiss Alisha".

Fear struck me and I blurted out. "I don't know what I'm doing. What if I suck at it?"

Chuckling he lifted my chin up. "Just follow my lead. I'll teach you everything. Picture how we use to kiss".

He bent lower and I could feel his warm, minty breath on my skin as I closed my eye's, then it happened. The shrill buzz of his doorbell shattered our first kiss moment. Alarm shone in his eye's. "Hurry Alisha, get in this coat closet while I see who it is".

"What? Why?"

"It could be my dad or another coworker. They might recognize you and word get back to your dad. We don't need that trouble right now".

I understood and agreed as he shoveled me into the closet. I heard as he opened the door and then heard a female voice ring out. "What the hell is going on Evan. I haven't heard from you in weeks. Why are you avoiding me?"

"Cassidy" I heard Evan gasp.

WTF! Cassidy? The very same Cassidy who was a accomplice to Gabriel's murder. The beautiful and sexy Cassidy? What is going on here? Does this mean that her murdering boyfriend is back too? This can't be good, and God why is Gabriel talking to her, why isn't he shoving her out the door telling her to never come back, that it's over. Please don't let him be stupid enough to fall for her again.

Chapter 22

Hell's Bell's

Absolutely fucking amazing. I'm ditched in a closet while listening to my man have this personal argument with the cunt responsible for having him killed. My stomach clenched as I heard her purr words of love at him. It took all I had not to bust free of this closet that was enveloped with his scent and claw her eye's out.

Straining my ears as to not miss any of their conversation, I steadied my head against the door and listened. "I mean really Evan, what did I do wrong?" I heard Cassidy whine.

"Well for starters Cass, you have a boyfriend that your not willing to let go". Evan grumbled.

"Oh Evan, he's gone. I haven't seen nor heard from him in weeks".

Hmmm... I thought, does this mean the dirt bag wasn't sent back or is this hussy lying? Whatever it is, I hope Gabriel isn't fool enough to fall for it. " Please Evan". Cassidy begged. "Let's start fresh. I promise I can make it up to you".

"I don't Cass, I need to think about it".

He needs to think about it, I screamed inside my head. What the hell is there to think about you idiot. The bitch had you killed. "Okay Evan, I understand. I'll give you time, but before I go kiss me please".

Oh no she didn't. He had better not. Ugh... Why do I have to be stuck in some closet where I can't see a thing. I heard silence followed by a slight moan and smacking of lips. I can't believe him. I mean yea, Cassidy is very pretty in a artificial, plastic way. I doubt anything on her body was real, but can't he see past that for what she really is? What she did to him? She's in love with his money and not the man behind the suit. Finally I heard them say their farewells and the door close. I had to escape this closet before I combusted. Slinging the door open I stepped out like a warrior princess ready to battle. Stomping toward Gabriel, I shoved him in the chest. "Are you fucking deranged? Tell me you didn't buy into to her bullshit? Remember where it got you last time asshole".

"Cool your heels Alisha. I didn't know any of that was going to happen or that she was going to kiss me".

"Yea, well you sure as hell didn't stop it".

"What's that suppose to mean Alisha?"

"Exactly what it sounds like. You wanted to kiss her. If you hadn't you would had sent her on her merrily little way."

"Sorry. I'm just so confused now".

"Confused. Your confuckingfused. Didn't seem like she was confused when she was okay with her boyfriend killing you dumbass".

"Enough Alisha. I don't plan on seeing her again".

"Maybe not, but she plans on seeing you because you didn't put your foot down".

"What should I have done Alisha, please tell me since your so smart now?"

"For starters, I would have shown her right back out the door and told her to never come back. Instead you fell right back into her clutches".

"I did not. I was surprised and shocked, that's all".

"No dickweed, surprised and shocked is going through what I went through".

"Fine, okay Alisha. Your right. Your always right".

Uncrossing my arms I stalked to the door. Gabriel grabbed my arm. "Where are you going?"

"School" I replied irritability.

"Wait, what about our kiss?"

"You clearly are deranged, aren't you? Why would you think I would kiss you now after you just swapped spit with that gold digging, murderous, woman. I'm leaving now. When you've decided what you want and gotton rid of Miss plastic, you know where to find me. Until then stay away from me".

"Alisha don't". But I hurried on out the door. Yes I might be naive but I wasn't stupid. How could he do this, especially after knowing what Cassidy was about. It's like her beauty enchanted him and he could only think with his pecker. And why the hell am I crying? No, this Evan is nothing like my Gabriel.

School was a struggle for me today. Most of my time was spent thinking of Gabriel and all the Events. The teacher might as well have been speaking in tounges for all I pertained today. As the last bell rang I made my way quickly toward the exit. All I wanted was to get home, soak in the tub, and watch reruns of "shadow Hunters". Wallow in my own misery per say. Just as my hand reached for the handle I heard my name being called. Turning I saw Drew waving toward me. What the what, I thought. Why is he flagging me down. I've barely mumbled two words to him my entire existence, and wasn't he dating Cher anyways. The only plausible reason he could be hunting me down was he needed help on his studies. Yep, I was the go to girl for that. Finally he caught up with me as I continued to speed walk. "Alisha, slow down".

Slowing down just a fraction I groaned. "What do you need help with?"

"Huh? Nothing. I just wanted to chat?"

"Okay. Games over. Who put you up to this?"

"What are you talking about? No one, honestly. I just wanted to tell you that you look nice today".

So yea, like I said earlier I did apply a bit more make up this morning as well as styled my hair but that was all for Gabriel. Not to attract attention from some over zealous, raging hormone, teen boy. Wait, I am a teen again myself. Ugh... this is all so hard. "Thanks" I muttered.

"Can I offer you a ride home?"

I was about to decline when I saw Gabriel sitting in his fancy smancy Porsche waiting on me. Nope, I can't deal with him yet. Looking at Drew, I gave him a wining smile and batted my eyelashes, because that's what I'm suppose to do right? And like silk the word's rolled off my tounge. "That would be lovely Drew".

As I slid into Drew's car I saw Gabriel glaring at us and I flicked him off. Thankfully he pulled off in the opposite direction from us.

Chapter 23

Blown Up

What the hell have I gotten myself into? My main reason for coming back was to set things right, change my life, and get the girl of my dreams, which was Alisha. When Alisha showed up on my doorstep this morning my heart skipped a beat. We talked and it seemed like I was gaining ground with her finally. The moment I'd been waiting for was just about to happen. My lips neared hers and the scent of lavender and honey assaulted my nose, then my door buzzer blared. True, at the moment I was shocked at seeing Cassidy and yes, I shouldn't have allowed her to kiss me. Alisha was right, I should have sent her on her way, but Alisha was so wrong in her assumptions and jumping to her own conclusions. I wasn't seeing Cassidy as some hot chic that I was dating. I wasn't thinking with my cock like Alisha had implied. I actually saw Cassidy for what she was.... a selfish, self-centered, piece of scum. Cassidy's looks didn't do squat for me anymore. The only reason I allowed the kiss was because I was in utter shock. My mind was running wild from memories. I was worried her boyfriend would bust in at any moment ending my life again. Then Alisha was all up in my face not giving me time to explain, not understanding the turmoil in my head at seeing Cassidy again.

After Alisha stormed out it all came rushing back full force and nearly took my breath away. I had a full fledged panic attack. One things for sure, if Cassidy reappears I will shut her down. Later that evening after sorting my emotions out, I knew I needed to apologize and explain myself to Alisha. After picking up some flowers I made my way to her school to await her dismissal. Spotting her rushing out I was getting ready to pull up beside her when some freckled faced boy grabbed her attention. I wasn't close enough to hear their exchange but it must have been good seeing how Alisha hopped into his old Buick. She spotted me and sent a firey look my way right before she shot me the bird. Typical older Alisha right there. My first instinct was to chase them down and toss school boy over a bridge, but I kept in mind that he was only a kid.

No, I had other plans for Alisha. What she fails to realize is that I'm a grown man. I won't play her games and I make sure I get what I want. Right after midnight I parked my car across the road from her house and once I was sure all was quiet I crept to her window. In a moment I had her window lifted and was inside her girly room. Tip toeing to her door, I locked it. Last thing I needed was her dad interrupting us. Walking to her bed I stood over her watching as she made that adorable chewing motion in her sleep. Eventually, I pounced on her like a cat. Her eye's flew open with alarm and I clamped my hand over her mouth before she could scream. "Calm down, it's just me" I assured her.

Once her breathing slowed and she realized I wasn't some intruder I slowly pulled my hand from her mouth. Venomously she hissed. "What are you doing here? I told you I didn't want to ever see...."

I brought a abrupt stop to her lashing word's by slamming my mouth down on hers. At first she fought me but I wasn't going to relent. Eventually she realized that and started kissing me back. Remembering this was her first kiss I softened the pressure from my mouth and made sure it was all a first kiss should be. Judging by her tight grip on my neck and suttle moans, I was doing my job. The kiss started heating up and I allowed Alisha to control it. When she pressed for more, I gave it to her. Becoming braver she started running her hands down the length of my back and intertwining her fingers in my hair forcing my mouth closer, making the kiss deeper.

Due to being loss in everything that was Alisha, I subconsciously started doing what was natural. Taking my hand I ran my palm down the silkiness of her stomach until my fingers skimmed the top of her pajama bottoms. I delved my fingers underneath the band and felt the soft material of her panties. Gasping, Alisha pulled her lips from mine. "No Gabriel".

Ugh.... The most hated word by men. To men hearing no was worse than a root canal, but I would respect her decisions. Grudgingly, I slipped my hand away and rested my forehead on her chin willing the pain in my balls away. Shutting my eye's tight I grimaced against the pain and heard a faint snicker come from Alisha. Lifting my eye's to meet hers, I asked. "Something funny?"

"I think your getting what you deserve"

"Oh you do now?"

Laughing through her answer she chuckled out. "Yes."

Giving her a fake mad look I removed her bottoms before she could stop me. "Gabriel, no. Stop".

Grinning slyly I said. "What's wrong baby? Your just getting what you deserve".

Quickly I ran my finger over her most sensitive area which caused a knee jerk reaction from her. "Gabriel, I promise if you don't stop I'll"

Cutting her off by inserting my finger into her wetness I arched my brows and asked. "You'll what?"

As I noticed her face become flush and her breathing growing heavy, I retreated my finger and left her hanging. "No, no, Gabriel. Please".

Laughing I sat up. "Not today babe, but I promise when I give you your first orgasm it won't be like this".

She sat up folding her arms across her chest clearly upset at my antics. "I'm mad at you anyways and not because of this. I mad over the entire Cassidy ordeal".

She was so cute setting there that I tweeked her nose and eased her worry. "Baby you have nothing to worry about where Cassidy's concerned. I was just bamboozled by her this morning. It had nothing to do with her looks or me being in love with her. That ship has sailed. Can't you see Alisha? It's you I want. It's you I love. You take my breath away".

I seemed to have left her speechless so I rose to leave. Bending I placed a gentle goodnight kiss to her lips and made my way to the window. Before I stepped out I looked over my shoulder. "It would be in that boy's best interest if you stayed away from him. Don't let me catch you with him again".

Before she could say a word, I slipped out and secured her window. Just a matter of time before Alisha's all mine.

Chapter 24

Breathless

After Gabriel left I sat on my bed running my thumb over my kiss swollen lips. What in the actual fuck just happened. Gabriel basically broke into my home and literally forced himself upon me. Not that I'm complaining, it was hot and would definitely go down in history for world's best first kiss. The thing that was bothering me though was his last word's before he left. Gabriel came off as threatening and I didn't know if he would actually make good on his threat. He left before I could explain my actions. Drew was just a over hormonal eighteen year old boy, not yet a man. I barely knew him and had no intentions of started up any romantic relationships with him. My only reason for hitching a ride with Drew was to avoid Gabriel. This was definitely a side of him I've never seen. Gabriel seemed so territorial and controlling where I was concerned. He did make me realize I wasn't playing around with some wet behind the ears boy, but a grown experienced man that was use to having it his way.

True, I knew that Evan wasn't the greatest human before his second chance here on Earth, but now that he knows the outcome if he doesn't change his ways it seems he'd be walking on egg shells. My worry now was that the Gabriel I know want be able to conquer Evan's harsh ways and return to his old self. I mean, yea, he's become a better boss and helping the needy, but can he keep Evan from resurfacing. Maybe I should talk to him about this before it gets out of hand. I knew it was late but this couldn't wait. The sooner, the better.

Crawling from my warm blankets I slid a coat over my pajamas and slid into my rainbow colored, polka dotted rain boots. Not exactly making the greatest fashion statement but the winter in San Francisco could be harsh and I knew it had started raining. The last thing I wanted was wet, frozen toes. Tip toeing from my room, I eased my dad's door open and carefully swiped the car key's from his dresser. I left a note on the kitchen table explaining that I had a extra early school project meeting and didn't want to walk in the fridgid rain. I'm sure he would agree and take the bus to work.

Once across town in the upper class section I felt a bit inadequate as I parked my dad's old bucket of rust amongst all these fortune one hundred cars. I snickered as I thought back to a childhood game of spot the object that doesn't belong. It would definitely be my dad's hoopty. Pulling my coat tighter to me I made my way to the parking garage elevator and punched in Gabriel's floor. Standing at his door, I buzzed and waited several moment's. I figured he was asleep so I allowed for some extra time. Eventually my patience started wearing and just as I was about to buzz a fourth time I heard the locks unlatch. Gabriel opened his door and fire coursed through my veins at the sight of him. Wearing only a pair of briefs, bed head, and sounding rugged as all get out, I could only gawk. My eye's was zeroed in on his briefs that proudly outlined his package. Grinning lazily he said in his sleep gruff voice. "See something you like?"

Clearing my throat, I tore my eye's from his manhood and walked in. Taking my coat off i laid it on the back of a chair and tried to blow warmth into my hands. "Here baby, let me warn you".

Coming closer Gabriel pulled me into his arms and his skin was ablaze. Within seconds I was thawed out. "Coffee?" He asked.

Nodding my head yes I decided to just get it over with. "I'm worried about you Gabriel".

Looking over his shoulder at me he asked. "Why. I'm fine".

"No, I don't think you are. Look I know the stories you told me about Evan before you returned and I swore I saw a glimpse of him tonight when you sent that threat".

"What threat baby?"

"Gabriel, you know clearly what threat".

Walking toward me he placed his hands flat on the table and leaned toward me. This man was positively gorgeous as I watched his abs protrude that led down to that sexy V right before it came to his.... snap out of it Alisha, I scolded myself. Giving me a knowing smile he replied. "Look I'm still a guy and I don't enjoy seeing boy's move in on what's mine. It was just a normal reaction that any hot blooded male would make. Call it jealously, protective, or what you will. Stop worrying babe, I'd never return to my old ways. Just keep in mind, I am human again and I will make mistakes".

Breathing a air of relief I nodded. "Okay, I feel better now. As far as Drew goes, I barely know him and I only took him up on his offer to avoid you".

Gabriel stalked slowly toward me like a lion. Taking his hand, he tilted my chin up until our eye's met. "Never avoid me Alisha and never except anything from another guy. Understood?"

What and how he just said that sent a uneasiness up my spine but I decided to blow it off. No need to continue arguing right now. "Since your here babe why don't we go cuddle in bed, you skip school and I'll bail on work and we can hang out all day?"

I had never skipped school in my life and I knew I should say no but Gabriel was right, we needed alone time together to figure our relationship out. "Okay, but we sleep, nothing more".

"Whatever you say babe" and I followed him to his bedroom. I know it's odd sense technically we have already had sex so I can't understand what my deal is about it now. Maybe it's the fear that he'll compare me to the other Alisha and conclude that he doesn't love this younger, shy version of me. Maybe I want add up to the older Alisha. My worries evaporated soon as Gabriel's arm wrapped around me and pulled me in. All was right with the world until we were woken by a thundering crash. Both of us bolted up and Gabriel looked at me with a knowing in his eye's. "Hide Alisha and don't come out no matter what happens".

Frozen I watched as Gabriel eased from the room to investigate. After a moment I realized I just couldn't set here and do nothing. Tip toeing from his room, I eased down the hall where I could hear voices. Peeking around the corner my biggest fear stood before me. There was Cassidy and her psycho boyfriend standing there with a gun trained on Gabriel. This can't be happening again I inwardly sobbed. Then their words penetrated my thoughts. "ALL you got to do is write me a fat check lover boy and we will be on our way. You want be harmed and you'll never hear from us again".

What the what? This doesn't make since. Either this go around was different or Gabriel had lied to me over the circumstances of his murder. All I could do was look on in terror.

Chapter 25

Exposed

Something had told me this was bound to happen again, just a niggling feeling I guess, but this time the sceniro was much worse. Alisha was here and hopefully she took my advice and hid. It was bad enough that I feared for my life but to fear for Alisha's life as well was heart pounding terror. Not only that, I worried she could hear this conversation and conclude that I hadn't been totally honest about my murder. I mostly hid it from her due to shame.

The truth was that this douche bag wasn't only Cassidy's boyfriend but her pimp as well. That's right, Cassidy was a high dollar call girl that I met at a swank bar one night. At first I didn't know she was a hooker. Cassidy seemed well educated, beautiful and dressed in the latest fashions. She definitely didn't look hooker material. I ended up in a hotel room with her that night and you could imagine my surprise when morning came and she demanded that I owed her two thousand for an entire night. Of course I refused her payment, I was livid but at the same time something about Cassidy had captured me. I couldn't get her out of my mind so I hunted her down. We started a whirlwind love affair and I was convinced that her feelings for me was as strong as mine for her. Many times I begged her to just quit, run away with me, I'd take care of her, but that bastard ruled her with a iron grip laced with fear. During our time together I never paid Cassidy for her time. However I did buy her gifts and whisk her off to tropical paradise's, but I was just doing the typical boyfriend thing, spoiling my girl.

That's what led to this moment right here. Cassidy and I had a argument once again about her leaving the streets and she fled from me back to her pimp ass boyfriend. I did love her but I finally realized she was just using me for the gifts and trips, so in away, yea, I was paying for her time. Anyways she told her boyfriend about our relationship and he didn't take it lightly. He saw it as money he was owed for my time with Cassidy. Busting into my apartment he demanded thirty thousand bucks or my life. Sure, I had the money but I wasn't willing to give him nor her a dime. I was basically calling his bluff, I honestly didn't think he'd kill me and I was wrong. So wrong.

So now the story unfolds yet again and I need to be very wise in my choices. Honestly I didn't even know if he'd allow me to live even if I did hand over the cash. Trying to buy time to think, I said. "I've got the money but I can't get it until the bank opens".

He looked skeptical at first then jabbed the gun in my chest that's when I heard a gasp and I knew exactly who that gasp came from, Alisha. I squinted my eye's shut tightly and prayed they hadn't heard her blunder. I was crazy to even think that Alisha would have listened to me and hid. Cassidy and Matt, her boyfriend slash pimp shared a concerned look and I knew they had heard. Jabbing the gun harder into my chest Matt questioned. "You got somebody here man?"

Shaking my head I said "no".

Nodding his head toward Cassidy he snarled. "Check it out".

Cassidy strode out in search of the noise. I heard Alisha trying to skitter away then Cassidy yell back towards us. "He has a girl here".

"Bring her here" Matt demanded.

I heard a scuffle a knew Alisha was putting up a fight. Then I heard Cassidy yell "you bitch" followed by Alisha groan. A few minutes later Cassidy drug a fighting Alisha in by her hair. Alisha broke free and came to my side huddling under my arm. Cassidy had two vicious looking claw marks down her cheek and in that moment I was proud of my baby. Matt pointed his gun toward Alisha and hummed. "Well, well, what do we have here?"

Before I could answer Cassidy snarled. "Didn't take long for you to find a replacement did it? She's awfully young don't ya think Evan?"

A slimy grin crossed Matt's face and he took his gun and used it to open up the collar of Alisha's pajama top wider. Moving forward I growled. "Don't you fucking touch her you piece of shit".

Laughing he removed the gun and pointed it at me again. Looking at Alisha he asked. "What's your name cutie pie?"

"I'm not your fucking cutie pie". Alisha growled and I caught a glimpse of my older, rebellious Alisha. Good, she would need that extra attitude boost to deal with this mess. The mess I innocently sucked her into. Bending down into her face Matt hissed. "I have ways to break mouthy ass girls. I suggest you give me a name lest you find out".

"Alisha" she spit toward him like venom. Giving his greasy smile again he pulled her to the center of the room and proceeded to walk perverted circles around her sizing her body up. "Hmm m.... I could really make top dollars off of you". He mumbled mostly to himself.

Glaring at me he snarkly stated. "You have until twelve tonight to Gabrieler my money. In the meantime I think I'll take this little angel with me to insure my payment and no cops involved. Meet me by twelve at the old lumber warehouse down by the bay. Understand that if you aren't on time or fail to follow instructions she will be mine to do as I please."

Moving toward him he placed the gun to Alisha's temple causing me to stop in my tracks. "I mean what I say Evan. If she means anything to you be on time or within the hour she will be sold to the grubbiest customer I can find" .

My eye's found Alisha's and my heart ripped into at the fear in her eye's, knowing there was nothing I could do to save her at the moment. "Alisha baby, don't worry. I'll be there". Looking at Matt I threatened. "Had not a hair on her head better be harmed or I promise I will kill the both of you".

Grinning down at Alisha he whispered in her ear as she cringed. "Hmm... he's the protective type I see".

With that he slammed his pistol into her head rendering her unconscious. It was the only way to make sure she didn't cause a scene when leaving my building. Helplessly I watched as he tossed Alisha over his shoulder and left. Waisting no time I quickly dressed and grabbed all I would need to extract the money from the bank.

Chapter 26

Fighting Back

Why am I so cold? Why does my head hurt so? Cracking my eye's open I saw that I was sprawled out on a hard, cold, concrete floor. It all came rushing back then. I had been kidnapped by those want to be gangsters and was currently being held for ransom. Please Gabriel don't abandon me I prayed. What time was it? I knew he only had so long to exchange the money for me. There was no windows in this dank room so I had no inkling as to know if the sun was up or had it sat. I decided staying completely still was my best option. If they were here maybe they'd let me be if they thought I was still unconscious. That's when I heard a flick of a lighter and the flame alumanated the small space. Tightly I shut my eye's and fained sleep. I heard my tormentor inhale from their cigarette and the smoke assaulted my nose. Then my blood froze as I heard his creepy chuckle. "Oh, don't pretend sleep sweetheart. I saw you peeking".

I remained mute and still, wishing the floor would gobble me up. Anything but being here with him. "You know you only have two hours left before I sale you. Looks like Romeo is going to be a no show. That's fine by me though because you will bring in more dough than I could ever get from him".

It was like he got off in instilling fear in me and tormenting me further. I heard his shoes slide across the floor and peeked my eye's open to find him standing over me. "Do you know what my clients would love to do to you?" He taunted as I cringed.

I remained silent and pleaded with myself to not give in, don't let him scare you. Gabriel will come. His harsh voice scattered my pep talk. "Cassidy is gone to fetch me some grub. Sit up".

I refused to move which infuriated him further. Reaching down, he grasped my by my hair jerking me up. His grimy face was mere inches from mine that I could smell his foul breath and had to fight the bile that was creeping up into my throat. "Seems you need a lesson in listening. It's obvious that lover boy isn't coming to the rescue so I'll do the honors of breaking you in. Teach you the moves that will keep my customer's crawling back. Show you how to satisfy a man".

Panic seized my chest and I felt like I was hyperventilating. Before I could react he roughly shoved me to my knees. "Your going to enjoy this".

Unzipping his pants he inched closer to my face. My eye's frantically scanned the darkened room for something, anything that I could possibly use as a weapon. Hope crept into my soul as I spotted a lead pipe meters away. As soon as he unleashed himself in front of my face, I grabbed his member and twisted it with all my might. He doubled over groaning in pain while I scrambled for the pipe. Once I had my hands securely wrapped around it I held it back over my head and soared it against the back of his head. Relief flushed over me as he crumbled to the floor in a unconscious heap. The pipe made a clattering echo as I dropped it and took off like a marathon sprinter.

Not knowing which way the exit was nor wanting to take the time to find it I chose the nearest escape route.... A window. Just my luck, it was sealed securely. Taking my elbow I smashed the glass out and felt a searing pain on my forearm but I didn't care. My main priority was freedom and safety. Looking out, I estimated it to be at least a fourteen foot drop to the ground but that didn't stop me. I'd rather risk a hard fall than staying here. Counting my blessings I launched myself out the window and was greeted by the hard concrete. Sure, I was in pain, but there's was no time to inspect my injuries. Standing up on wobbly legs I scoured the property and noticed a torn spot in the chain link fence. Running over on obviously a twisted ankle I shimmied myself through the small opening scratching my back along the way. Looking around at my new surroundings I found myself on a lone driveway that must have been the main entrance to the warehouse. Deciding it would be best to stay off the road I hurried over to the wooded sidelines. As I trudged along I could feel stones sliceing into my bare feet as thorns snared at my exposed skin. Suddenly I saw car headlights approaching at a speedy pace and I hunkered down in the brush praying it wasn't Cassidy returning and that I was well hidden. As the car neared my heart skipped a beat as I recognized Gabriel's Porsche. Mustering up what ounce of strength I had left, I hurled myself into the middle of the road. I heard the screeching of breaks as the headlights blinded me. The Porsche cane to a abrupt stop right in front of me and I placed my hands on the hood while taking deep breaths.

"Oh my God Alisha" I heard Gabriel's voice as he exited the car and came to me. "Are you okay?"

My only reply was. "Get me the hell out of here".

Once tucked safely inside the car and several miles down the road I lost it. I cried until no tears was left as Gabriel held my hand and offered me his comfort. Eventually exhaustion overtook me and I fell into a deep sleep. I don't know how long I slept but when I woke I was in a comfy bed and had a clean t-shirt on.

Slowly I sat up and saw Gabriel standing by a window. "Where are we?" I asked through dry, cracked lips.

Gabriel rushed to my side and cradled me to his chest. "We are in Vegas. I had to get us as far away as possible because I'm sure this isn't over".

After a moment his word's registered and I went into panic mode. "Oh my God, my dad is going to be so worried. Why didn't you just go to the police?"

Tossing me his phone, he told me to call my dad and makeup some likely lie. "Why didn't you go to the police?" I demanded again.

Running a frustrated hand through his hair he spoke in a tired voice. "For many reasons Alisha. One being your dad would discover the truth about us. Another is I could also be charged with buying a hooker and my reputation smeared".

"But you didn't buy her Gabriel. You had no clue what she was when you met".

Sounding a bit harsh he bit out. "Not so easy Alisha. It's my word against theirs. Do you honestly think the law would believe that I would honestly date a prostitute and not composite for her time? Now call your father and be convincing".

A bit hurt by his reaction I numbly dialed my dad's number and made up a believable story about a last minute school trip to check out colleges. After we disconnected I felt so dirty for having lied to my dad. Standing I realized how fealthy i was as well as sore from my ordeal. "I'm going to take a bath" I announced and Gabriel only shook his head and said he'd order us some room service. My stomach grumbled at the mention of food. Within moment's I let my broken body disappear into the depths of the tub. Life would be so much easier if I could not only wash the dirt away, but wash the pass few day's away as well.

Chapter 27

Something's Got To Give

For two day's now we've been holed up in this hotel, only leaving for food and one short trip to the mall for clothes. I could see the strain on Alisha's face and knew this was getting to her. Many times she pleaded with me to take her home and report them to the police, but I can't do that, I'd be ruined. I also knew we couldn't continue to hide out. Alisha needed to return to school and her dad was bound to start questioning her lies. Not to mention I had a job waiting on me.

Our time together in this hotel room was anything but romantic. Mainly we argued about returning home and if we wasn't fussing we were tuned into our own world, shutting the other out. I hated how things was between us and I knew I was mostly to blame but my hands was tied and my options slim. Either stay on the run, return home and alert the authorities and risk jail time, or return home and pray they've let this go. Something had to happen and happen soon.

I watched as Alisha returned from the bathroom and started shoving items into a bag. "What are you doing?" I asked a bit astonished.

"What's it look like I'm doing Gabriel? I'm leaving with or without you. I can't keep hiding out. I've got school and this is my senior year. I can't keep missing day's. Not to mention I'm running out of excuses to tell my dad."

I reached her in one step and gripped her by the arms. "You can't just leave Alisha. Don't you understand what they would do to you if they found you".

"Yes, I do, but I have to go. If it wasn't for you I wouldn't be in this predicament at all".

And there it was, the fat elephant in the room. I knew she harbored bad feelings toward me for this situation. I fucking knew it. I seen the shock at her own word's register across her face. Gasping she mumbled sadly. "I'm sorry Gabriel. I shouldn't have said that. It's just this all has me so stressed right now and I don't know what to do."

Letting her arms go roughly, I stepped away. "No it's fine. If that's how you feel, that's how you feel. As a matter of fact I don't blame you".

Giving me a sympathetic look she said. "I don't feel that way. I'm just angry that's all. I have no right to take it out on you, but I do mean what I said. I'm leaving here today either way".

"Alisha don't be a idiot. Give me time to figure something out".

Frustration rioled up inside of Alisha and she let it rip. "I can't give you anymore time Gabriel. Only if you'd just go to the police and report this. I can prove I was kidnapped. I still have a lump on my head and marks all over me. I'm sure there's evidence still left at that warehouse. The longer you wait the less evidence we have. Please Gabriel".

"What part don't you get Alisha? If I report them I wouldn't only shame myself but my family name as well. I'm sure my name would be dragged through the mud and I could face time for buying a prostitute. Fuck, stop acting like a child. Think for once. Your dad would also find out about us because you would have to testify as well. Think. Alisha".

"You know what Gabriel, fuck you. If anyone is acting child-ish it's you. I'm trying to do the right thing, stop them before they do this to other's. As for my dad, I can handle that. You, your more worried about your polished reputation than you are anything. You know what? People make mistakes, it's allowed. So what if people judge you, they don't know the story. You'll bounce back. Plus you have the money for a bigshot lawyer to save you from jail or at least cut your time".

Glaring at her with concrete eye's I could only shake my head in disbelief. Alisha would rather I return and face the music instead of working out another solution. Maybe she was right, but that's a hard pill to swallow, knowing I could lose a lot of respect. Not just from my family but friends, my employees, other businesses. Fuck why can't she just wait and trust my decisions. She was standing with her arms crossed not relenting a inch. Finally she broke the dense silence. "I'm going home now and if you don't want to come, I understand. However it doesn't change my mind".

Biting the inside of my jaw to maintain my emotions I slowly shook my head. "I'm sorry Alisha. I can't go".

She nodded her understanding and grabbed her bag. "Could I borrow money for a bus fare at least?"

Digging my wallet out, I handed her a few crisp hundreds then turned to stare out the window. When the door shut signaling her departure I felt like my ribs caved in. Was this it for us? Is this how we end? My mistakes came back to bite me hard. We had ended before we was even given a chance to start. I hope I'm doing the right thing.

Alisha

I honestly can't believe him. He'd stake us for his clean reputation. Sure, I understand it would be a embarrassing scandal that would hurt his image and family name, but I was willing to sacrifice mine to do the right thing. I know my dad would be super disappointed in me and I'm sure classmates would gossip but after it was over Gabriel and I would be free to pursue our relationship. In the past few day's I saw the selfish side of him, the one he told me about. Was it possible he couldn't change like he vowed to.

I'm not going to lie, this hurts Like hell. I truly felt we was made for each other and I was looking forward to making the most of our second chance together. It's strange but we have this out of world connection due to our past. As I boarded the bus I took one last look at Vegas with a heavy heart hoping it didn't end like this. I felt like I had lost my only friend.

During the long ride home I had plenty of time to think. I knew my dad would be concerned over my bruised body and I came up with many explanations but only one sounded right.... The truth. If anbody, I could trust my dad. When I got home I would sit and tell him everything. Everything but the whole

Gabriel was a angel once and me a addict. No, I didn't won't to sound mentally unstable. I would tell him about my semi relationship with his boss and how he was being blackmailed by a old girlfriend and her partner. I would explain that I was there when they busted in and taken for ransom. Hopefully with my dad in my corner he would go with me to make the report. I hated to do this to Gabriel, but I felt this was the right thing to do. Those slime balls needed to be stopped before they can harm anymore innocent people. I just hope Gabriel realizes I'm not going against him, I'm not trying to hurt him, I'm trying to protect us. I just hope he'll understand my reasoning and forgive me.

Chapter 28

The Truth Unfolds

I sat across the kitchen table from my dad with tears streaming down my face. I had just finished telling him the sordid details that's occurred. He simply sat and stared with his chin rested on his hand in deep thought taking a deep breath he finally spoke. "Alisha I don't know what to make of this. You've always been one to avoid trouble. When did this thing start between you and Mr. Carmichael's?"

"When I met him at the company picnic".

Shaking his head he spoke. "Alisha he is a grown man. You have no business messing with him, besides I'm not sure his intentions are pure. Right now the main thing is to go to the police station and file a report. The sooner these creeps are off the streets the safer you are. We'll discuss your punishment later".

My dad rose to grab his jacket and it hurt to see the disappointment etched into his features. The ride to the station was quiet.

Once there I relayed the story and had pictures taken of my injuries. Sure enough they found evidence of my abduction at the warehouse. They also made me tell them Gabriel's whereabouts. I felt sick turning him over to the police but I knew this was the best thing to do. I just hope in time he would forgive me.

I couldn't believe how long we was kept there and I was exhausted. All I wanted was my bed. Finally they said we was free to go but a officer would join us and set outside my home until the culprits were caught. At least knowing that I felt somewhat safer. As we was walking through the lobby I spotted Gabriel being escorted in. Wow... they got him back in no time. Our eye's met and held each other. My dad stopped, wondering why I had came to a sudden stop. He followed my gaze and grabbed my arm trying to pull me along. "Let's go Alisha".

I shrugged from his grip and said "wait".

I hurried up to Gabriel with a apologetic look. "Gabriel I'm so sorry but I think this is best for both of us".

Gabriel leveled me with a stone cold stare. "Thanks so much Alisha. I'm just in for questioning right now, but I'm sure that will change".

"Please don't be upset with me Gabriel. I truly didn't mean to hurt you or bring you trouble, but honestly this is what needs to be done to stop them. They found evidence at the warehouse. This will work out, I promise".

With sarcasm he replied. "Please forgive me if I don't trust your word's".

That really got me deep and my eye's welled up with unshed tears. "Please Gabriel. Just give it time."

"Says the one who won't have to pay the price".

I shook my head in disbelief at his word's. This was definitely the Gabriel I didn't know. Seeing my distress my dad came over to pull me away. "It's time we go Alisha".

As my dad led me off I glanced at Gabriel one last time and mouthed "I'm sorry".

The next two day's was a nightmare. Between the cop's being parked outside my house and my dad I was never alone. I tried several times to contact Gabriel but my calls went straight to voicemail. My dad refused to let me out of his sight until those ass bags were caught. It was killing me not knowing what happened to Gabriel. I prayed and prayed they didn't book him. As I was at the edge of my sanity there was a knock at the door. My dad answered and in stepped a officer. "I'm here to inform you that your attackers have been arrested and will remain in custody until the court date. You will be notified soon with the date. In the meantime you may want to look into getting a lawyer". I could feel the stress trickle from my bones at hearing the news. Then he mentioned a lawyer and my glee vanished. There was no way my dad could afford a lawyer. Then another thought occurred to me. "What about Ga... Evan Carmichael's?"

"I'm sorry Miss, but I can't give that information out".

Nodding my head I watched as the officer took his leave. Turning to my dad I blurted out. "I have to go dad".

"Oh no you don't Alisha. You are to stay away from that man. Besides your grounded".

Those word's stunned me. Never had my dad grounded me. "What, why?"

"You know exactly why Alisha. Running off, lying, seeing that man. This isn't the child I raised. You'll see in time this is for the best. Besides we need to check out some lawyers".

"Dad you know as well as I do we can't afford one. Now please, let me go?"

Absolutely not".

Never had I disobeyed my dad but this time was different. He was interfering with matters of the heart. Swiping my coat up I looked at my dad and whispered "I'm sorry". Then ran out the door.

I could hear my dad calling after me but I refused to turn back. Finally I caught the bus and headed to Gabriel's apartment. As I laid down on his buzzer my nerves seemed to be zooming through my body like electricity. Finally after several moment's he swung the door open. "Go home Alisha".

"No. Not until you talk to me".

Before he could slam the door in my face I forced myself inside. "You can't stay mad at me Gabriel".

"I'm not mad at you Alisha. I simply just don't give a shit anymore".

"What's that suppose to mean?"

"It means that this is the end of the line for us".

"Really? I can't believe you. Just because you didn't get your way your ready to throw the towel in on us".

Spinning around to face me he growled. "No you did that when you ran your mouth. Your the reason I'm in deep shit".

"We couldn't keep running Gabriel".

"Just get out Alisha. My life is over, ruined, finished. All because of some fool girl I was infatuated with".

I couldn't stop the tears this time. His word's stabbed me to my soul. "You can't be serious Gabriel".

"My fucking name is Evan... Not Gabriel. You got what you wanted, they've been arrested, now kindly leave my premises".

I tried to think what the old, badass Alisha would do in this situation. Surely she wouldn't set and cry like a weak kitten. Conjuring up her courage and attitude I swiped my tears away. "No EV-AN" I made sure to pronounce his name as sarcastically as possible before I continued. "Your the weak one here. You know it's quite pathetic that you put more into your squeaky clean reputation than how you treat people. I'm not the fool, you are. If I never see you again it still be too soon. Have a nice life rolling around in your money...alone".

With that I turned on my heel and strode to the door with my head high. There was a hideous statue that sat on a pedal stool by the door. Taking my finger I gently toppled it over sending it crashing to the floor. I fained a oh no look. "Oops, I'm so sorry, but it does look better now".

"Real fucking mature Alisha".

Shrugging my shoulders I sauntered out feeling free. I had finally found that Alisha.

Chapter 29

Time Will Tell

Day's turned to weeks and weeks into months. The case was slow moving but finally our first court appearance was upon us. No, I haven't heard or saw Gabriel since the day I waltzed out of his apartment with my head held high. Yes, it hurts but I've made my peace with it. This is how he wants it, this is how it will be. His loss right? But, yea, on my low day's I wonder if maybe I should've fought harder for us, maybe I shouldn't have turned everything into the cop's, maybe I was wrong and he was right. But in my defense I was scared and worried, something had to give.

I can't say my life has went back to normal because I'd be lying. Sure, my dad finally let up off me, especially when he learned that Gabriel and I was history, but my social life hit a all time peak. Once my story aired on the news and was splashed in every newspaper from here to Antarctic, I became small town famous over night. Suddenly all the popular girl's at school wanted to be my bestie and all the guy's wanted to date me. I guess they thought since I snagged the city's most eligible bacholer, playboy millionaire, future business tycoon, I was a big deal. I was the "It" girl. I could wear my panties on my head and swear it was the latest fashion rage and the next day every girl would walk into school sporting their knickers on their head. None of this went to my head though, actually it irritated me to no end. I'd just politely smile, decline any party or date invitations and be on my way. It's amazing how shallow some people are. When I was a shy nobody, they didn't know I existed, once this case was revealed along with my romantic relationship with Gabriel I was suddenly their Queen.

Sadly things were the exact opposite with Gabriel from what I can tell. No, I haven't heard anything directly from him so my only resource is the media, and we know how the media loves to twist the news around to form a juicy story. In most articles Gabriel was painted as this hideous monster that bought hookers and prayed on younger women. They claimed he blew his money on lavish trips and material possessions. That he has been apart of Chicago's party and drug scene since he was eighteen. They couldn't be further from the truth. Every time one of those hackling reporters caught up to me they always questioned me about him. I never revealed anything other than saying he was generally a good guy and this was all a big misunderstanding. Well needless to say that choppy ass reporter twisted my word's and claimed I was under Gabriel's spell. How laughable is that? Really, where do today's journalist get their degrees... The stop and shop on buy one get one free day?

I feel bad for Gabriel and how his name is being slandered but there's nothing I can do and I know he points the finger of blame at me. I guess he's right though, it is my fault, I did however turn him in. My only hope is years from now, when all this has faded away he can forgive me. Meanwhile school is coming to a end on a few weeks and I've been accepted to the University of Illinois with a full blown scholarship. Yay me! Thankfully I'll be just a few hours from home so I can check in on my dad. I'd feel much better if he'd just start dating. At least I know he won't be lonely. My other concern is that this trial will drag along and interfere with my schooling. A non profit lawyer snagged my case up due to the glamorous Carmichael name attached to it, but I'm not complaining. That took care of my biggest worry.

I nibbled on dry toast this morning, honestly my stomach couldn't even handle that. Today I would lay eye's on the rotton scum that kidnapped me as well as seeing seeing Gabriel since this all blew up. My stomach was one sip of tea away from being the next natural catastrophe. My lawyer prepared me for the onslaught and possible brutal questions the defense attorney would throw at me. Including questions of my sexual encounters which were void, previous boyfriends which was nonexistent unless you count Theo, a boy from my imagination I schemed up at fourteen so I didn't look like such a loser to my classmates. My school records would probably be drug up which they was squeaky clean and perhaps the effect of my mothers death had on me. That was my only concern. I could handle anything they threw my way, but I don't know how I will handle that. The object is for them to make me look bad, lead the jury to believe I'm a crazy young woman and possibly have mental issues, that I'm lying and try to play head games with me in hopes I'll stumble up. I just hope Gabriel will speak well of me whilst he's on the stand and not seek revenge for exposing us.

My dad bought me a nice dress to wear today. It was simple with a flowery pattern that boasted innocence. Once we stepped from the car, I smoothed the wrinkles down and held my dad's hand as if I was five again. My teeth worried my bottom lip as we entered the court room. Flashes from camera's half blinded me as I was led to my seat. Great, they allowed the media in, why wouldn't they. This was a scandalous trial involving the biggest name in town. Once seated I shyly glanced around. The jury was a colorful bunch. Young and old, male and female, a great mix I guess. Then I spotted whom I assume to be Gabriel's parents. They both reeked of money and sophistication. His mothers eye's held mine for a split second and I could read the disdain that was there for me. Moving on along I caught sight of Gabriel's many power lawyers sitting next to my one measly pro bono lawyer, but no Gabriel. That quickly changed. Suddenly flashes started blinking off as Gabriel made his entrance.

Within a moment he was seated less than six feet from me in a impeccable suit. Shyly I glanced over under lowered lids and offered a weak yet scared smile. Gabriel didn't give me anything back, just a quick glance then turned his attention elsewhere. Wow, never in my life had I felt so small, so insignificant, then I did right now. I felt tears burn the back of my eyelids and begged them away. I could really use some moral support right now and he basically shooed me off like a pestering fly. Clasping my hands in my lap, I pretended to twiddle my thumbs as I stared down at my shoes.

All too soon we were told to rise as the judge made his entrance and the proceedings began.

Chapter 30

Your Up

I sat in uncomfortable silence as this began. I listened to the lawyers represent their case separately. By this time I had worried a raw spot on the inside of my lip. I watched as Cassidy was called to the stand. She settled on the bench in a fit of tears. First, her lawyer questioned her.

"Is it true you had a love affair with Evan Carmichael's?"

"Yes".

"Where did you meet Mr. Carmichael".

"At a popular club. I was leaned against the bar when he approached me and asked to buy me a drink".

"Had you been drinking before he came over?"

"No Sir".

"Did you drink when he offered and if so how much did you drink?"

"Yes, I did. A glass and a half of champagne".

"Would you consider yourself to have been intoxicated?"

"Heavens no".

"Was Mr. Carmichael intoxicated when he joined you?"

"Very much so. His speech was a bit slurred".

"Did he continue to drink afterwards?"

"Yes, about four beers and a shot of tequila".

"Did you make him aware that you was a prostitute before you left the club with him?"

"Yes, I let him know as soon as he offered to buy me a drink".

"So it's very possible that Mr. Carmichael was too intoxicated to recall you telling him that".

"Yes".

Gabriel leaned up to his lawyer and angrily whispered. "She's lying through her teeth".

His lawyer hushed him and said quietly. "We will have our turn".

"The night you and Matthew supposedly broke into Mr. Carmichael's home what happened".

"It was all Matthews plan. I had been joining Evan on several trips, dinners and such but he refused to pay me. I was coming up short on money so I explained to Matthew the trouble I was having with Evan's payments. Matthew lost his temper and he... and he". Cassidy pauses to dab her fake tears and compose herself.

"It's okay. Take your time".

Cassidy finally continued. "Matthew said if I didn't take him to Evan's apartment he'd kill me, so I was scared for my life and I took him. I had no idea what his plans were".

"What did you do when he took Miss Staley against her will?"

"I begged and pleaded with him. I said she's just a young girl".

I felt vomit hit the roof of my mouth but managed to quell it. That lying sack of shit I thought. The bitch laughed and encouraged it.

"Thank you. That's all the questions I have at this moment".

As her lawyer sat down mine rose and took center stage. "Your honor, I only have questions pertaining to Alisha Staley".

"You may go ahead".

Nodding, he walked over to the bench toward Cassidy. "Is it true that you and Alisha had a altercation before she was knocked over the head and taken against her will?"

"No, not at all. I mean she freaked out a bit when Matthew busted in, but no altercation".

My lawyer grabbed a envelope and looked at the judge. "May I present these photos to the court?"

"Permission granted".

He held a rather large photo up of Cassidy taken on the day of her arrest. There, in her cheek was my scratch marks. "How did you receive these. They was taken the moment you was arrested. Three day's after Alisha's abduction. Did you or did you not chase Alisha down the hall of Mr. Carmichael's apartment where you attacked her and drug her by her hair into the living room where everyone was and in defense Alisha managed to scratch you?"

"Oh, ummm, well. It wasn't like that. Not at all. I was merely trying to calm Alisha down and she went crazy and attacked me".

My lawyer held the picture up for all to see.

"Did you taunt Alisha over her relationship with Evan. Was you jealous and perhaps wanted Alisha removed from the picture and Matthew could do that for you".

"Fuck no, I wasn't jealous over that little bitch". Cassidy erupted.

The judge beat his gravel and shouted. "Order in the court".

My lawyer apologized and said he had no further questions. Cassidy just blew her act by her perfect outburst. Next Gabriel's lawyer's basically shredded what was left to Cassidy's sob story. Before I knew it court was released for lunch and I would be taking the stand next. Needless to say I couldn't manage to hold a cracker down.

Upon returning I prepped myself as much as possible and as my name was called my palms started sweating. My lawyer was first and he made it bearable. Gabriel's lawyer's had no questions for me so theirs was up next.

"So tell me Miss Staley what's a young girl like you staying with a older man and on a school night as well doing out?"

"Evan and I had a silly argument earlier in the day and I came over to patch thing's up".

"Was your father aware you had visited Evan?"

"No".

"So you snuck out".

"I wouldn't call it sneaking. I am eighteen. Legal adult". Ha. Take that asshole I thought.

"Is it true that Mr. Carmichael's is your father's boss?"

"Correct".

"Could your relationship with Mr. Evan's be due to the fact that he has money and to help either your father's career"?

"Absolutely not. My dad wasn't aware of our relationship until this took place".

"Tell me Miss Staley. How many sexual partners have you had?"

"None. I'm a virgin".

"So are you saying that you've never slept with anyone, not even Mr. Carmichael?"

"That's what I'm saying".

The lawyer looked at the judge. "Permission to have her examined by a doctor Sir?"

"Objection" my lawyer cried out.

"Over ruled. Permission granted".

Well that sucks balls I thought. This crumb of a lawyer tried to berate me at every twist and turn but I managed to outsmart him until he brought my mother into this. "Miss Staley is it so that you lost your mother at a young age?"

"Yes".

"Is it true that for a time afterward you gave your father trouble, became a problem child so to speak. Intentionally beat up class-mates, lied on your teachers and fellow students when you was reported. Finally your father had to seek a therapist to as it you with your violence and lying".

I cringed on the inside for it was true. This is something Gabriel never knew. It was apart of my life I had buried. Against my will the tears spilled over as I answered.

"Yes, that's true, but I was only eight and dealing with the loss of my mother. After receiving help my behavior went back to normal and I've never done anything like that since".

I don't know what was said next because the tears wouldn't stop. The judge finally ordered for a break so I could Gabrieler myself. I rushed from the court room and escaped to the near-est bathroom where I could fall apart in private. Eventually I calmed down enough and splashed cool water on my face. Once composed I went to the break room for some water but stopped when I saw Gabriel in there with his parent's. Quickly I spun around on my heel and opted for the water fountain. After taking in several refreshing gulps, I stepped outside for a bit of fresh air. A few moment's later my dad stepped out and told me it was time to resume. Taking a deep breath I braced myself for round two.

Chapter 31

Completeness

After two grueling weeks, many arguments presented, evidence turned over, the trial came to an end. I was elated that it was over yet saddened at the same time. Once I leave this court room that's it, I'll never see Gabriel again. I thought about approaching him one last time but I couldn't muster the strength to do so. This trial had taken a lot away from me. I was forced to be examined then have the news of my virginity announced in this room full of strangers. I had been belittled, humiliated, ripped to shreds and I needed to heal emotionally. If I was shot down by Gabriel again, right now, I would lose what composure I had holding me together. Instead, I held my head high and marched from that room, not sparing a glance in his direction.

It was my time now. Giving the things that has happened to me, that being lessons learned from older Alisha as well as younger Alisha, I have learned a lot. I've really growed and matured. Wise with age I guess. I've discovered my strengths, what life means, and the importance of being true to myself. For the first time I was no longer scared, I didn't care if I was seen as the nerdy girl, the ugly duckling. I was me and I was coming into my own.

Once home my main mission was to knock out these last day's of school then set my aim on college and my goals. Thankfully I would only be a few hours from my dad which I think was good for both of us. Summer flew by and I did work fulltime at a book store to earn some cash for things I'd need. The day my dad dropped me off at my door I busied myself by settling in my room. I had just hung my last poster on my wall when in walked my roommate. I guess you could say I was star struck by the way I was staring, Extra tall and super model slim, wavy brown hair along with a outfit made of money. Pulling my dumb look off my face I introduced myself. "Hi, I'm Alisha Staley, your roommate".

My nerves eased when a bright smile crossed her face. "I'm Lea. I'm sure we will end up the best of friends".

We chatted a bit and got acquainted but I finally told her I was going to check out the campus. Soon as I open the doors and stepped outside I scanned the grounds and inhaled the newness. Turning my smiling face to the blue sky I remembered my promise to myself. I was in a new place. No one knew of my court scandal, I wasn't the nerdy girl who turned popular by my abduction. This was my new beginning. I could be whoever I wanted to be. Skipping off the steps I headed over to all the club booths and before I knew it had signed up for a few. Look at me, being all social and shit. I also made a few new friends and decided that I would use some of my summer earnings and buy a new wardrobe before classes begin. New year, new me.

With the advice of my new roommate Lea, we hit the town. By that evening I had more hip duds and chopped my long hair off pass my shoulders. I now sported a blunt bob with fringe bangs. Walking back onto campus I noticed quite a few male students turn their head. That's right, my time to shine.

Often Gabriel and our time together wormed it's way into my head but I refocused my thoughts quickly. I came to terms with the fact that he was done with me, that he considered my betrayal unforgivable. It will always hurt simply because we share more than the normal couple bond. We basically share a futuristic bond, a heavenly bond. I'll never regret any of it though. Gabriel brought so much to my life and saved me in many ways just as I have saved him. Soon as the trial was finished and those sorry excuse of humans found guilty the Carmichael name shined again. The tarnish was polished away and Evan glowed in his lavish reputation. He still remained a good boss but I know nothing else about him. Is he seeing someone? Does he miss me like I do him? My dad refused to discuss him most the time and I wasn't about to question my dad either. I've put him through enough. Within the first few weeks I started dipping my toes into the dating ring. Nothing serious, just a few different guy's to catch a movie with, go grab some sushi, or just hang out. I was excelling in my studies and life couldn't be better. I also landed some part time work at a on campus coffee house. Dad sent me money weekly but I know he needed it. Before I knew it fall break was upon us and I was headed home for the holidays. The day before Thanksgiving dad sent me out to grab a few missed ingredients but I ended up finding a lot more.

Me being me headed uptown to splurge on a fancy holiday cake for my dad. Just a little something to show my appreciation. Choosing the best one I made my way to the door. With my hands full with this cake I was fumbling with the door and before I knew it, the door was getting ready to slam back on my fingers. Shutting my eye's I sucked in air as I braced myself for the pain sure to come. "Whoa there". I heard a all too familiar voice. With my heart pounding I looked up and sure enough it was Gabriel.

"Alisha" he said somewhat shocked. "I had no idea it was you. Your hair, you cut your hair off. It's looks good. You really look good".

"Thanks" I mumbled as I fought with the huge cake box. "Here, let me get that". He said taking the box from me then he laughed. "Wouldn't be you if you wasn't getting your fingers smashed".

Giving a small grin I said "yea, nice save there...again."

I immediately knew my mistake soon as those word's left my mouth. "I'm sorry". I reached for my cake. "I really better get going. It was nice seeing you".

To my surprise Gabriel raised the cake high out of my reach. "Alisha let me carry it to your car".

Nodding my head I mumbled "okay. I'm just parked around the corner".

Gabriel followed me and secured the cake in my car. "How have you been" he asked.

"I'm doing real good, thanks. How about you?"

"Just working all the time".

"Yea me too. Well I work at a coffee shop on campus".

His eye's lit up. "You went. That's great. I'm happy for you".

I couldn't place my finger on it but Gabriel seemed different as well. Almost jolly it seemed. Gone was the usual snarky attitude. He was carefree. "Yes, and I'm loving it".

"Judging by your looks it's loving you back. You really look good Alisha".

Our conversation seemed to go silent and I don't know what overcame me, maybe my new fearless ways but I leaned up on my toes and pulled his face down to mine. None to gently I pressed my lips to his. I hadn't kissed him like this since his Angel day's. Breaking away I glanced up at him and knew he still felt it. Giving a smirk and a wink I opened my car door and slid in. "I'll be seeing ya".

I left him standing there as the year's first snow flurries started to drizzle down.

Chapter 32

Visitor

The Holidays flew by all too fast and before I knew it I was back at college. It was hard to believe that my Freshman year would be over in a few months, but I had really grown. My first week back was rough due to having so many day's off but eventually I adjusted. Friday Lea invited me out to a party with a few other's just to blow off some steam. I half heartedly agreed to wear a tight black dress that Lea tossed at me. Once ready we met with our other friend's and headed outside after wrapping up in coats. We barged outdoors in a fit of laughter and chatter. It was already dark and the wind was whipping. Dead, crisp leaves whirled through the air casting eerie shadows to dance around. Something odd yet familiar caught my eye. Stopping I trained my eye's and and spotted him walking away briskly. Even though his back was to me I knew it was him for I caught a glimpse of shadowed angel wings. Yea, sounds crazy and maybe it was, maybe it was the wind blowing the street light that caused the effect, but I saw them. "Hey Lea, you guy's head on, I'll catch up. I forgot something".

Lea nodded and skipped away with the other's. I took off in the direction where I spotted Gabriel. Almost catching up to him I called his name. "Gabriel?"

He froze but never turned around. I slowly approached him and said his name softly to his back. Taking a deep breath he turned around and looked so sad and lost. "What are you doing here?"

He seemed nervous which was so unlike him. "I, um, I wanted to see you but you seemed to be busy so I took off. I didn't intend for you to see me".

"I can't help but to see you Gabriel. Something is still there with you and I always know your presence. Always. You might be human now but some of the other things remain".

"Yea, I know. I'm always warm, extra warm. I should let you get back to your friends".

"No". It came out almost like a squeal. I didn't want him to go. "Let's do something?"

"Like what"?

"I don't know. Maybe go for sushi?"

"That's fine but I insist on driving. You look cold and also very good in that dress".

Smiling I followed him to his car. Once inside he went to blast the heat but I grabbed his hand stopping him. "No Gabriel. I want you to warm me up, like old times".

Before he could answer I crawled over to him and stradled his lap. I placed my arms around him and laid my head into the crook of his neck. His warmth immediately enveloped me as he wrapped his arms around me. In this moment everything felt right, safe, and I knew I was where I was suppose to be. Gabriel started to speak and his voice was low and thick with emotions. "Alisha, I'm so sorry for how I treated you. Plea..."

I didn't need to hear anymore so I cut him off by pressing my lips to his. I knew without a doubt I was ready. Shock sprung to his face as I quickly unclasped his belt and started to work on his zipper. Yes, I was about to lose my virginity in a car, but that didn't matter. What mattered was the here and now and the love I had for this man. Once I freed him I worked myself free of my panties. "Alisha wait, are you sure?"

Grinning I said. "It's not like we haven't done this before, well in another time anyways". We both laughed and I continued. Looking out the window I spoke to no one in general. "If our angels are still here now would be a good time to disappear, stuff is about to get real".

Gabriel and I both saw a flutter of leaves suddenly and knew our angels had taken our word for it. Laughing together over our shared secret, our shared experience, and our shared knowledge of life and death we met each other's lips again. Slowly I lowered myself down onto him and pushed pass the pain. In this moment our beating hearts and souls was the only thing that existed. There was no time, no regret, no sadness.... Just a deep love that could be felt omitting for each other's bodies as we became one.

It didn't take long for Gabriel to lower the seat and reverse me to the bottom. I traced my finger along the scars on his back, evidence of his once beautiful wings, but he was still very much an angel. His skin still glowed during our passionate moment and the gold flecks in his eye's shined brightly, not to mention his skin was a incubator of warmth. Yes, my Gabriel still had some angel DNA.

Afterwards we held to each other for awhile then made our way to eat. Like two love sick teens we huddled together in a booth sharing words of love and hope and couldn't keep our hands off each other. In the end nothing else mattered..... not my dad, his parent's, our age difference, money, or our current locations.

What mattered was us and that after all we had been through we had finally found the people we had been the day I first saw him.... my angel, my love, my life.

Yes, by all means, we were truly a match made in heaven.

CPSIA information can be obtained
at www.ICGtesting.com
Printed in the USA
LVHW081249101122
732762LV00014B/831